December Alliance

Other books by Annie Aaron

A Whisper of Springtime: Jason's Heart Transplant Miracle
Irrevocable Impact
Oh Mother! Oh Father!

Also look for these forthcoming titles!

Joseph
Sadie Spider Does Lunch

December Alliance

This story happened before cellphones and Internet

ANNIE AARON

ARPress
ILLUMINATING IDEAS
EMPOWERING VOICES

Copyright © 2020 by Annie Aaron.

ARPress
45 Dan Road Suite 36
Canton MA 02021

Hotline: 1(800) 220-7660
Fax: 1(855) 752-6001

Ordering Information:
Quantity sales. Special discounts are available on quantity purchases by corporations, associations, and others. For details, contact the publisher at the address above.

Printed in the United States of America.

ISBN-13:   Softcover   979-8-89389-170-6
           eBook   979-8-89389-169-0

Library of Congress Control Number: 2024914622
Printed in the city of Canton, MA.

Dedicated to Mr. Craythorne

CONTENTS

JANUARY 23

My dear wise counselor, advisor, and friend Sophie:

Today, the twenty-third day of January on a Tuesday in this New Year, I'm ready to begin a long letter to you. I want to write at length to explain why you haven't heard from me for over a year now. From the depths of my heart, I want to help you understand what my life has been over the "quiet period." Or shall I say the hard times, the terrible times, and the glorious times which evolved month by month out of my life over events that came before. Ah, yes, that is true of all that has occurred. And, in fact, so much has transpired, I hardly know how to summarize all the events for you. Regardless, there are some things I want to tell you right now and some things I will tell you later.

But first of all, let me tell you how much I enjoyed flying to St. Louis the last time to see you. St. Louis is a wonderful location. And with my living here in Tooele (incidentally, I met a woman in St. Louis who knew that Tooele was just outside Salt Lake City, but pronounced my town the funniest way. I finally taught her to say

"""

Tew-ILL-uh.) But back to my point, I still miss the teeming life that one finds in St. Louis. And, speaking of St. Louis, I want to know if the art center you built with its wonderful grounds and community for the many artists living there is properly appreciated. I think that it is a holy answer to the problem that people have today of searching for a place where they can be both spiritual and aesthetical.

I want to be a spiritual person, as you know, but I want to be an aesthetical person too. And it is a great struggle to finally understand that in some ways, indeed, "truth is beauty and beauty is truth" as Keats said just before he died. And he was only twenty-five years of age! Surely, there is a great deal of beauty in truth and truth in beauty. That is why I always want to be close, at least in spirit, to the art center that you built and to be one of the artists who belongs to your community. I wonder about the elderly gentleman that I met there. He was writing a book regarding the spiritual aspects of marriage. Has his health improved? I was inspired by his lofty ideals and dreams.

While I'm reminiscing about your art center, I am thinking about the three-story building where you live. I remember that the old house seemed very cold the last time I visited you two years ago. Of course it was wintertime. I remember the night the wind howled at the windows and how I felt as though the panes would shatter. I remember hearing the sound of the blowing wind, the rumbling of the wind. And I remember how I never thought a place could be so cold. But that is just a memory that comes to me now.

I'm sitting in my living room, that same living room where you visited me a couple of years ago. It had been such a wonderful experience to have you here with me, to see the maturity and wisdom with which you graced my home and my life. You said at that time how overwhelmed I was to realize that you took me very seriously, that you cared what happened to me and that you cared about my future. You saw what it meant to me to realize that you truly cared about my spiritual well-being and, in fact, my whole purpose of existence.

So, I'm sitting in that same living room holding fond memories of you and I am writing to you. In fact, being here in the living room helps me focus on you and makes the writing easier. I feel confident and productive as I sit comfortably using a TV tray as my writing table. It is very quiet by the way. My two boys are gone for the day—something I'm grateful for. Not that I don't miss them, but quite frankly, every adult needs a little private quiet time to think on the adult aspects of the problems he or she has. Well, of course, you know that. I suppose I mention this because it's just now that I'm beginning to see the truth of the idea.

I must point out that early on, I wanted to visit you in order to tell my story. As each event came to the resolution that it now has, I actually thought about calling you. But then I realized that I had too much emotion to contain myself. I say that it could be overwhelming to me to have to speak out about everything I had endured. I believe that now with a little quiet and calm, I can pace myself writing you about at least those events which have transpired within the past three months.

I suppose now, that I must begin to tell you the story that I wanted to tell you. First of all, it may surprise you to know that I have just come back from a stay at the hospital. So you see, it is going to be a long time, many words away before I fully explain the hospital stay to you. So, let me begin by telling of events that most recently occurred. I'll begin with last Tuesday on January 16.

That day, I left Tooele at 3:15. I went to the van, fastened my two boys in, got into the driver's seat was ready to take off. Speaking of cold weather and cold places, I must say that it has been very cold here. In fact, I remember sitting there under the steering wheel surveying the vast chilled landscape around me. The snow lay deep and silent on the hills to the east above Pine Canyon. But I knew the roads had been cleared and I had heard on the radio that no snow was evident on the highways or interstate. No weather problems I told myself and we started off.

Anyway, we headed toward the city, just a half hour away. In fact in a little while, I could see the Great Salt Lake to the west standing mirage fashion with Antelope Island looming monster-like out of the water. Really, it looked very much like the scene in the blurred photos one sees of the Loch Ness monster, one of the unexplained mysteries of life.

But I drove on. With the overcast sky it was hard to see where the lake ended and the sky began, steel gray merging into steel blue. But quick enough, I got a glimpse of Saltair standing like some forgotten sentinel keeping guard out in the desert. Anyway I drove on, veered right on I-80, motored onward to Salt Lake City.

As I was driving, I began thinking of the news I had to tell you. Big news! Still, I couldn't bring myself to actually take time, sit down and write. Now, my friend, I've gotten to that point and I want to tell you of things that had transpired since last November.

To start off, do you remember Mrs. Cunningham? The lady who lives next door to me? I must tell you how on that morning of January sixteenth, Mrs. Cunningham had sat in my living room listening to me talk and talk. I was encouraged by being able to discuss with this neighborly friend some of the things that had been on my mind. I must add that as she listened and listened, I was beginning to feel as if life could go on for me. It had to go on. It would go on with our without me.

Ben, my youngest son, and Mr. Cunningham were building clay figures which again seemed like frightening monsters. Not that I was seeing monsters everywhere, but I was basically in a frightful state. Anyway I was driving in the van and I was thinking about the various things I wanted to tell you. I knew at some point I would write to you, because I had things to tell you. But as each day passed, there had been more and more things that I had to weave together to explain, things of great import. The task seemed overwhelming.

Anyway, still driving along that afternoon, I caught a brine-shrimp smell that pierced through the mists from the lake. It was a disagreeable odor and it made me cringe. Like the reaction you get when someone scrapes a blackboard with his fingernails. It set me on edge. What if this smell were the odor of my failures, I was feeling that I should be doing more. For the first time in months I was beginning to think maybe I could cope with where I was and what had happened. The part I have not yet told you about.

I was certainly feeling that I was up to going to Sugar House to see my sister and her three daughters. Thus, this is where we were going last Tuesday afternoon. Driving along, I even felt that I looked half-sane, so to speak. And considering these points, I was driving along confidently and thinking of details of my life that I might soon be revealing to you. Now I realize I am implying many things but bear with me. Let me proceed with the first event!

That day, while driving, I glanced in the car mirror and caught a view of my sons in the back seat. There was brown-eyed Ben yawning, his hair overgrown, he obviously needing a hair trim.

And there was Shane, ever the dreamer, looking at the cars we were driving past. At that moment Shane wanted me to sing a song for him. I switched off the radio and started singing a French lullaby. The boys sang along, happy enough to have something to do. For myself I was filled with so many thoughts I could not express then and am still not ready to express now. But let me remind you that there had been numerous times that I have felt fear, fright—like a woman who'd awakened from a nightmare.

But I drove on singing with my boys for a while. Then, I was aware I was singing without my chorus. I looked around. The boys had fallen off to sleep. I guess listening to the hum of the engine and the cadence of my voice had lulled them away. At this point all was quiet. I fell back into silence, driving; driving and remembering things.

Remembering things like my sister JoEllen being nine years older than I and being creative and helping me. She's always been a big help to me. Big sister Jo, you know how proud I was of her. I'm sure you recall the many times I used to refer to my youthful days with Jo and all my siblings. As children we did so much talking, giggling, and planning out intricacies we wanted to have in our lives.

But driving on, I began thinking of my brother Steve and the mischief we used to get into. We were playful, all right. Yet, Steve, Jo and I were often talking about ideas. We would often look up quotes by famous poets and other interesting people. I remember Steve quoting Thomas Jefferson who had said something along the lines that, "It is a fool that gives up freedom for security." That particular quote seemed to penetrate my thoughts at that moment.

Anyway, thinking of my youthful days, I began thinking about my boys. Maybe my boys would never experience all the kinds of mental exercise my siblings and I had had back when we were young. I wondered if they were old enough to think about what Mr. Patrick Henry had said, "Give me liberty or give me death." My boys often seem lonely. Perhaps they were lonely for the excitement of understanding and discovery. I truly wanted to make that up to them, but it was and is a hard, hard job to do all alone.

Next, I glanced out the side window, caught a glimpse of bare maples in a row lining the street where Jo lived, with that, realized I was nearly to my destination. I reviewed my happy feelings to be driving to JoEllen's. There was Jo's dance production that she was doing for her girls this week. The idea of having my nieces perform for a large audience always created an air of excitement for me, and all. JoEllen certainly is an oasis for my boys. They can feel the artistic spirit and desire to explore that she has. And I can feel it too. I'm always grateful for JoEllen.

Also, there were JoEllen's three girls. These girls really loved my boys and wanted to teach them exciting new things. In fact, the girls were old enough to take the boys around to places like the Children's Museum and the Planetarium. This was all possible because Sandy was old enough to drive

Truly it does seem impossible that all three of Jo's girls were born before I married John, which was seven years ago. Grown up so fast! The years have moved along so fast in this regard. Yet in other ways the years have plodded along. I'll tell you more about that later.

But speaking of JoEllen's girls, I can't give her all the credit for the loveliness of her life and the way she has raised her children. I have to acknowledge Nick too. Nick has been a very good husband and he has been the right husband for JoEllen. He loves theater, for example and he goes to see whatever is playing in Salt Lake City.

They can't do very much traveling right now, but they certainly do try to see whatever is produced in Salt Lake and they do take the girls to see theater productions when it's suitable. Nick even tries to include me every possible time

For example, I had wanted to see *King Tut: the Musical* which was playing last summer. A fabulous national troop was in Salt Lake City. Nick had gotten tickets for both John and me but John had more important things to do. Thus, Sandy and a girlfriend went instead. To tell you the truth that had hurt. Too often I had forfeited tickets that were gotten for me and John. Tickets had been given to others who were "really interested in the arts." I always hoped that John would go, but he never wanted to attend. He did not care for what I considered "marvelous productions."

But to continue, that day, when we arrived at Jo's house, the boys and I hurried to the door and went inside. We were met right away by JoEllen and her girls. Janet and Patty took our coats, the boys and I fell into open arms of Sis. We were hugging and headed into the kitchen, everyone talking and talking. Sis had fresh-baked cookies and steaming mugs of cocoa. We consumed the wonderful refreshments while smacking our lips from eating the delicious treats.

Somewhere during our conversation, JoEllen asked about my husband's family. She was very concerned as to how John's family was taking things. Later you'll understand the meaning of this statement and she also wondered when I'd be going up to Idaho to visit Mother.

And as I've said, seeing Jo with her three daughters reminded me of my youthful days. Memories stirred in my mind as I briefly reflected back to when Kathy, Jo, Steve and I had spent many hours together talking and dreaming. But, this day, I was at Jo's house. We were the parents with children and had grown up matters with which to concern ourselves.

Perhaps one of the nicest things that transpired on this visit was that, Sandy, JoEllen's eldest, as I've said, asked about my photography. She mentioned some shots I'd done at Flathead Lake in Montana and at Yellowstone. And I really appreciated that. Sandy is a very sensitive girl. I had to thank her for remembering my interest. I think you should know now that there have been precious few who have been interested in my photography work. And that I have always enjoyed photography and capturing on film, the things that surround me, however simple they may seem. Yet, my husband John was the least interested of all the people in the world. He always criticized me for spending any money on film and photography projects, ignoring the fact that I received pay for my work and was able to reimburse him for the advances he gave me. He simply wanted none of it. Even when I showed him a check with my name on it, it made no difference. And this was just the way of John. Truly, I had taken great photographs of Flathead Lake and the surrounding area. Also, just recently I had sold a number of reprints of my work. I am sure that my work had value though never to John. Well, you'll hear more about this later.

But, there at JoEllen's house, we visited for as long as I thought we could. Then it was time to go, though all the cocoa and the cookies had not been consumed. I told the boys to hurry up and said to Jo, "You know how much I wish you success in your latest venture and I'll be glad to take the costumes or whatever that you have to the other little girls." To which Jo said, "Wonderful." We embraced. Then Jo gave me the costumes, and the boys and I were gone.

Once we were again en route, we headed toward Taylorsville to leave the first costume, next we went on to West Valley. Quickly enough we had delivered all but one costume. To deliver the last costume, I drove up one of the surest routes to get to Magna on Thirty-fifth South, a route that would take me right to my destination. And now begins the tale of the mad adventure that followed.

The moment I turned onto Thirty-fifth, I saw that an orange Chevette was following me closely. I noticed that the driver was a young man and that he looked angry. Not too pleasant an observation, but that is what I made of it. I was driving forty miles per hour in a forty-five mile an hour zone and thought perhaps that was why he was angry. But, I couldn't speed up. There was a car in front of me, a silver-haired driver barely doing forty and this was a "no pass" zone. I didn't want to provoke this impatient young man, but what could I do?

I took a glance in the rearview mirror and I saw that the now irate fellow was trying to catch me eye. So, I gave him my attention. And he made an obscene gesture. Well, not to be intimidated, I turned my mirror away from his image. But I could feel his anger. I could feel it growing and growing. I could feel him getting closer and closer.

Finally, I rearranged my mirror, glanced back and saw that he had begun motioning me to hurry up! I was quite angry now, downright mad. "Who is this?" I yelled to my car. "Is he a psychopath?" Then I called to the back seat. "Shane, write down the car license of the man behind us." I got a pen off the dash, tossed it back to Shane.

He caught the pen and I saw him whip around, write down the license number. "I got it down Mother," Shane said. Shane always carried a notebook. Wherever he goes, he had his notebook with him.

Ben was chewing his fingernails. I could see that he was alarmed. His eyes were big as saucers. I continued to drive with what I could only call "the maniac" behind me. I wanted to get away from him by driving faster. He was beginning to frighten me just as he was frightening my boys. I couldn't understand why he was doing this.

I looked out of the van and there was a grocery store ahead. I told the boys to hang on and I made a quick left turn. I thought perhaps if I turned off the main road the man would give up the chase. I turned so quickly that I didn't give a signal. With that, the man swerved in right behind me and turned up the street following me very close indeed.

There was no doubt that he had a malicious focus on my car. And I didn't know why. The thought struck me to turn off into the first subdivision. I thought perhaps he wouldn't follow me into a subdivision. When I came to the next street, I turned right. He followed. I made a U-turn to get back to the main road. He pulled up to the side of my van and cut me off. He leaped out of his car. I don't know if I can express the startle and the shock to me of this action. What is this? I asked myself. Did he want a confrontation with me? Why? Why? My thoughts were a jumble.

Suddenly I remembered John's hunting knife. He always kept it in the glove compartment. I fumbled for it. I couldn't let this madman get inside my van, kill my two boys or kill me! He could be a strangler! Perhaps he had a gun. I had to struggle to keep a cool head. At that instant, I could see there was enough room to pull around him. I threw the knife onto the passenger seat, gunned the van, and screeched easily past his car.

The man jumped back into his car, gunned his motor and was hot in pursuit of me. I got a good look at him. He had blond hair and a very red face. He wore Levi's was medium-tall. But what could I do? I had no phone or I could have dialed 911.

I bore down on the gas feed, my hands stuck to the wheel. I tried to think rationally, but what I felt was panic! *What could I do? Knife him? When? How? Stone him? Look for stones? Look for the police! Keep your eyes on the road!* I told myself.

I drove like the panicked person I was. I felt that I had to protect myself and my boys. Who was this monster? I continued to ask myself. Sick questions filled my head. Sick answers muddied my thinking.

As I pulled out from the subdivision onto the main road, I nearly hit a woman with a baby in her car. I gunned the van, hit Thirty-fifth and headed to the only place I knew where police hang out.

His car turned, followed me going east. He kept driving with one hand like a man searching for something under his car seat. I don't think I've often been willing to kill, but now I felt that I was. I told my boys, "Keep you heads down and pray."

They had to be frightened. I knew they were frightened. They didn't answer back. They didn't ask questions. It was terrifying. It was as though a local horror story had come to life and I was the victim. Nightly I'd read about lunatics in the newspaper and watched on the evening news, stories of motorist's cars ramming other cars. For example: a person getting killed for cutting someone else off on the freeway. It's a tension and a madness that pervades our world. I've seen it so often on television, on the news—people who kill for no sane reason at all or people who kill because they're angry. They are angry at everyone about everything. I didn't know what this man was angry about. Possibly, he didn't like the color of my van. The boys like the van, maybe this totally red-faced stranger did not.

I was sweating through my knit top. I felt that I was in a desperate situation. Deeply stressed, certainly! I felt overcome by fight or flight instincts. I shifted the van into overdrive. Finally, I saw a red light. There was a red light at Fifty-sixth West. I pulled to a stop. There was a wretched pain shooting through my head.

And like that, right there at the stop light, the man got out of his car gripping a handgun in his fist. Green light! I floored the gas pedal, lurched straight ahead, the wheels of my car sounded across the roadway. He dived back into his car, screeched away, turned up Fifty-Sixth Street heading south.

"Thank the Lord," I sighed. "Maybe he's giving it up!" I needed that reassurance. My heart was pounding against my coat. Still I kept driving fast hoping to see a policeman, hoping that one would stop me. I was doing sixty, surely one would stop me and report me, then, I could report this man. My legs were jelly and shaking. I saw a police car coming my way, it was coming my way, but then it turned off, I couldn't see where. I kept on driving. I headed for the police station—kept on driving. At least I knew where I was going on this main road.

Once I got to the city building, I told my boys, "Get out now!" We bolted the car, hopped the steps, got inside, I shrieked, "I need POLICE!" Some people, no uniforms, drifted my way. I saw no police. Where were they?! A policeman finally showed. He was walking toward me as in a slow motion clip. He was eating a candy bar.

"Good grief," I called out at him, "Listen, I've been through hell!" I was panting and couldn't stop. I tried to tell my story, but the words had to fall out in between the pants. I could not stop them. I panted out the license plate number. My boys panted when I did. I was drenched in perspiration. It had soaked clear through my coat. I was cold too. I shivered. My boys, wide-eyed, shivered also. I sank into a nearby chair, Ben on my lap, Shane gripping my hand.

The policeman sat at a desk, started filling out a report. "What's your name and what's the complaint and so on. Give that in order, not all at once," he told me.

I pulled myself together, went through the story in the order he had given. He finished writing. "Okay, we'll check it out," he said. "But let me say this, you can go on home now if you want."

"Oh no," I insisted, "I'm not going home until I find out about who this lunatic is." I couldn't believe what the policeman was saying to me. My whole body felt as if it was collapsing. I was near to faint.

"Are you okay, lady?" I heard him say. But at that moment, everything went black.

Well, there's so much to tell about this, Sophie, but I must say that this one event changed my thinking about many, many things. Just the event of being chased, I mean. I know, believe me, that all people have experiences that change things for them. After that event, they see things differently; they put them in a different context. They can anticipate different outcomes as a result of the experience. But this experience was MY change. Look, let's admit one thing about me, I had gotten in the habit of evaluating my life according to how safe it was. This is the first time I saw that I had this habit, that I really saw it clearly.

I was always expecting optimum security. I know that now. You know me, I wasn't supposed to have any losses. You know, I had shut myself off from possibilities and my potential to expand my horizons. We talked about it even. If you want me to put it back into the terms that we used then when we discussed it. I had closed off my ability to make my understanding fit with my real existence. I no longer observed myself observing myself.

With this experience that I have just told you about, I realized I had this shortcoming, one of my many shortcomings. I simply hadn't seen it within myself. But yesterday, I looked in the mirror and I said, "I'm worn out and tired and not invulnerable and I will never be." And I gave a little sniff and thought, *I made it this far. I might not have.*

As you know, we both have changed. When we met in college, I was fired up with knowledge. I wanted to succeed, to do something to change the world. I was ready to think on a higher plane, you know, the one we learned about, a form of *carpe diem.* A type of artistic *carpe diem* and a kind of spiritual *carpe diem*—to let go of the material world, the grasping world, the pin-it-down world and to move on to a world of lofty thoughts and lofty aspirations. But how I turned out is another story. I see now that all I wanted for so very long was simply to be safe and to stick with sure things. That wasn't me was it? It couldn't be me.

You know that I was always a dreamer. I am a dreamer. Tell my Sophie, that this is true. Tell me it's not dead in me. Tell me even after this crazy horrible, wild experience and my being so shocked to discover that I wasn't safe, that something could have happened to me, physically, socially, in my practical existence. And you can say, "Naturally you're upset. Naturally you were shaken and then collapsed with the realization of what the experience meant." Tell me that I can overcome this fixation with security, that I can take a chance on my dreams. Can you tell me it's not all over for me? Tell me that I can find a new way!

Sophie, I realize that we've talked about this subject many times. We've talked about the raw power that was inside of you and inside of me. We talked about how we can construct things, how we can invent, we can create, we can do something with what we have in our intellects, with what we finally understand. It's too easy to accept all the disappointment, all the mediocrity, all the stupidity even. It is too easy to accept being ordinary.

Being like everyone else takes no real effort. Yet, it's hard to be extraordinary, to do what I'm talking about now. I mean it's hard to hike off with a big torch in your hand holding it up high while saying, "Hey, I'm going to be lighting the path for you and me, Sophie, and for anybody else we know who can see the fire that we hold."

Oh, I don't know. When you analyze the real understanding and you say, "I've got this real understanding." You know it's very much like owning a treasure box, but it's buried deep underneath the floor behind the house in the cottage that hasn't even been built yet that no one's put a foot in. But if you set your box of treasures, your dreams, high on a closet shelf out of view, who are you? Your secret closet shelf, where you never see it! You could only pull out your treasure box once in a while to convince yourself that you hadn't missed out in life all together.

So to the questions, should I take a chance? Should I hope again and live for my dreams and forget about security? Should one ever try that? As I look back on my life now, I realize that I never did do this in early times. I wasn't a risk taker. But, I'm an adult Sophie. I'm supposed to be able to chart my own course. I've said that over and over and over, but I didn't see what I was really saying. I didn't see that if I was going to develop the lofty dreams that I had, if I was to experience those things I really wanted to experience and understand, I was going to have to work very hard. I could see that life was going to be very risky and very difficult. I would have to separate myself from the masses of mediocrity surging in on all four sides.

Truly, I have hesitated about writing to you, about telling you of my experiences. It has been difficult to share even this first of my stories. But there is so much more involved than being frightened by this man. It was horrible enough. However, I should now proceed to another point. I'll try to give you a little more background. I'll go back a little ways and tell you of a couple of months past. And I'll describe where I was then in my thinking, my meaning, my mind set, my psyche. This is what I mean about the phases of my thinking. Thus, I have to tell you now about an encounter that I believe will eventually help to bring all of this to clarification. And that will bring me back to the point of asking this question: *Do I really want to dare to seek my own dream?*

I must close for now my dear friend. I'll explain more later as I find the time.

As always, Anne

WEDNESDAY JANUARY 24

Dear Sophie,

It's another day and I've taken up my pen again. In fact almost twenty-four hours have passed since I was writing you before. But my line of thinking is still the same. All of the moods and the problems and the implications that I referred to before are still with me. Remember that I told you I wouldn't attempt to tell my whole story all in one spurt—nor would I even try to tell first things first. All you know so far is what happened with the man who followed me in the car and how it upset me so much that I passed out. Anyway, that much of my story you are now aware of. My next burden is to get the rest of the story told in the best order I can manage.

Well, let me start by saying that one of the things I did this morning was to take some exercise and move some heavy furniture. Naturally that has made me very tired. And, of course, I shouldn't have pushed myself so hard. At this moment, though, I know I really must keep on going, and I mean that at several different levels.

But I also must take a moment to describe the atmosphere. Right now I'm looking at the rain through the big front window. It has been raining and raining. For two days now, it's been raining. Everything is wet down with the rain, washed away. And, moreover, the trees are leafless, except for the Scotch pines. You remember the pines I'm sure. And the few evergreens we have along the block. There are a few old dead ragged leaves which have blown over from Mrs. Cunningham's peach tree which was the three that loomed so large right next to the sunny spot by my house. Also, there's the large sycamore tree in my yard. Do you remember it? Today it stands stark and naked against the somber sky. But one day soon it will be different. I can hardly wait to see it green and full of life when summer comes. Today it is bone-chilling winter but tomorrow will bring a change.

And change is the theme of the next episode I will relate to you. I am going to tell you about a meeting that has changed my life. You'll find out how later on. But for now, here follows the story of a meeting that occurred before last Thanksgiving.

To proceed, last November, shortly after Halloween, it was raining just like today, cold and rainy. I waited till Shane came home from school and then I put the boys in the van, hopped in, and off we drove to the local grocery store. We were soaked from the moment we first stepped out. I wasn't thinking of doing anything except a quick spree of grocery shopping and then getting back home and making dinner before John got in from work. John was still working in Salt Lake in city planning and was always ready to eat once he arrived home. Anyway I'm sure I told you about his job at city planning. He had worked there for at least five years.

Anyway, as I said, I know we'd be drenched going to the grocery store in the rain, but something pulled me there, some unseen force.

To recall the complete event, on the way to the store Ben promptly fell to sleep while Shane told me about his day at school. Shane told me that at school he had learned about some early Utah pioneers. I, in return, told him about some of John's people who settled Tooele back in the early 1850's. John had already told the boys these stories so many times but of course they enjoyed hearing about their ancestors.

I began with tales of some of John's progenitors which included three brothers who settled in the Tooele area. They were from Europe and one of them was a great musician. I'm sure I told you about these people and their early misfortunes. You recall don't you that I told you how incredible John's particular family and, in fact, many of these early Utah pioneers were. I wonder if I would have been able to sacrifice my comfortable home and earthly possessions and on top of that make a commitment to travel such a long distance all for the purpose of being able to worship in a way that felt right to me. Obviously it took real conviction and courage on their part.

The pioneers really believed in a God who cared about them as individuals. God lead them here to the Great Salt Lake, a place where they could receive revelations, build temples, and create a family unit whose members would care and watch over one another.

In reply to this information, Shane said, "Tell me about Grandpa Tuttle when he had holes in his moccasins and how he had to walk through the snow to get help." Now, I don't recall telling you that story, so here goes. The main goal of the early Utah pioneers was to live in an area that would allow them to worship God as they pleased. They chose to be free of anything that impeded their true nature. And of course this issue has been an important one to me for a long time. The pioneers took a great chance in taking the course they did, and though I have never done such a thing, I can admire it and be inspired by accounts of it.

But to continue, Grandpa Tuttle, one of John's ancestors four or five generations back, was a key figure in settling Tooele. Grandpa Tuttle came to the Great Salt Lake with the first Latter-day Saint pioneers. His company had left Nauvoo, Illinois. And that part is very interesting to me, because, as you know, I grew up in Illinois around Chicago and yet I'd never heard of the Latter-day Saint Church until I met John. This company of Latter-day Saints persisted through many trials. They simply said, "We're going west!" and they did just that. It's amazing to imagine that they followed through on their search for this free space that we talked about. Then too, many of them died along the way. What a risk to take! That was really facing insecurity; taking off across the continent like that, hoping to find the thing one valued far greater thing than being secure.

Anyway, among John's early progenitors, several of their company died of cholera their very first week after crossing the Mississippi River. They traveled up and down the plains, valleys, and mountains along the way. His progenitors had come clear to Wyoming in covered wagons and stopped at Fort Bridger where I suppose his Grandpa Tuttle got his last pair of moccasins at the trading post. Grandpa's company however, was running later than expected into October and got caught in a blizzard before they made it to the Great Salt Lake Valley. Grandpa Tuttle being only 21 years old, and strong, was asked to walk to Salt Lake to get help with one other member of the group. It required traveling many miles on foot through patches of snow, to reach their destination.

Grandpa Tuttle had holes in his moccasins and had to stop once in a while to take out the rocks that got inside. His long walk into town was broken only by these pauses as he recorded in his journal along the way.

Well, telling this to my son Shane, he wondered why Grandpa didn't have any hiking boots. I explained that there weren't any stores along the trail. But Shane, of course, couldn't imagine that. "A place where there wasn't any malls, grocery stores, or fast food places? How could that be, Mama?" he asked.

I tried to explain that point to Shane along with the fact that Grandpa Tuttle and a fellow pioneer had to alert local authorities about their stranded situation. A shoemaker who recognized Grandpa when he arrived in town, told Grandpa he could have shoes ready for him in two days if he'd take time to be fitted for a pair of sturdy proper ones. The shoemaker evidently was all too familiar with the trail Grandpa had walked. The best thing about this story is that it really happened. As I explained to Shane, when you talk about fortitude, isn't this a magnificent example?

Well, now, Sophie, I must pause again. You won't believe it. I just glanced out the front window. The rain has stopped! I can even see a little patch of blue through my window. Oh, I'm thrilled! I wish you could be here to share this kind of lifting of the spirits I feel. One tiny act of nature and a person like myself, can feel exalted and exhilarated. I don't have this feeling often. But I have it now and had it once I had gotten inside the grocery store, which is the part of the story I have started telling you.

As I said, due to the rain I really didn't want to go shopping. I had to force myself to leave my warm dry home. But once the boys and I were inside the store I was glad I'd gone. I pushed my shopping basket up the aisle. As I was selecting fruit in the produce section, an older man came right up to my cart. I was putting a bag of bananas in my shopping cart and here was this gentlemanly looking fellow.

He blinked through his spectacles, raised his brows and said, "Nice weather, this rain." It wasn't a question. He obviously liked the rain.

Shane's eyebrows had shot up. He didn't appreciate the rain because he couldn't go outside and play. And I usually didn't like the rain either. But this gentleman went on, "Bee-u-tee-ful day." He stuck a thumb beneath his coat under the strap of his bib overalls. He then adjusted his wire rim bifocals and he winked at Ben with crystal blue eyes seemingly undimmed by age. His bushy eyebrows stood at attention.

His facial features were in constant motion as he launched into a one man act. "My dear young lady, have you heard the song about Tooele water?" He took off his workman's cap to reveal silver wooly hair sprouting out along the circumference of his head. In addition, there were a few strands crisscrossing atop his shiny scalp. He made a swipe across his forehead with the back of his hand. That's when he launched into singing:

> Oh the water here in Too-il-lee
> It sure is full of minerals
> Oh the water here in Too-il-lee
> It's plum full of radiation.
> Oh the water here! Oh the water here
> Is sure enough to kill ye?"

Sophie, you'll never know how embarrassed I felt at that moment. You know me; I don't like to create a scene. My ears became feverishly hot. When he began singing, I stood glancing around the store to see if anyone had heard. I wondered how they could NOT hear.

His booming baritone voice filled the entire store, but no one was looking over my way. *Good*, I thought, wanting to escape quickly. One normally doesn't just sing in the grocery store in Tooele. You remember about Tooele, it has about 14,000 people in all. Everyone seems to know everybody else. I certainly knew everyone at the store on this particular visit, everyone including a good many of John's relatives. But this man wasn't known to me or really anyone else I'm sure. He was a free spirit and that was a shock.

As he wrapped up his song, he deftly selected some bananas, weighed them and put them in a sack. At the same time, Ben and Shane moved closer to me, grabbing on to the produce sacks I was putting in my cart. Seeing this, the man said to my boys, "I sure like seeing young men helping their mothers." Ben smiled at the idea. Shane straightened his shoulders a little. This gave me the opportunity to take a closer look at the man and his basket. I could see that this fellow had some carrots, bread, and spices in his shopping cart. Yet, he was dressed like a man who'd been working hard all day. I decided I had to try to find out more about him without judging him. In fact, I was convinced that it was impossible to easily judge him. He was a one of a kind.

I tried thinking of a question I could ask him. Very rarely are there strangers at the market in early November. I didn't know if I should put it that way. I certainly couldn't say to him, I want to know what you're up to and what you're all about. I couldn't exactly say to him, "What do you know about Tooele that I don't know? And what about this radiation? Do you mean radon? Or arsenic floating through the air from industrial mills? Or nerve gas from the Army

Depot?" Oh, heavens! I know that living in Tooele we have more than our share of environmental problems to consider. But did the man know about these things? And did he know more about these things than I?

Finally I asked him, "Are you from this area or just passing through?"

His face was animated as he replied, "Can't say as I am, Miss, from around here that is. My good Mother and Father named me Walter Wellington and I am originally from Iowa. I'm related to the movie star Wellington, but don't let him know." His face held hardly a wrinkle yet had the look of days in the sun, with a dab of peach high on his cheek bones. He had a twinkle in his eye as he spoke and he certainly was captivating. At least I was captivated by him.

Sophie, it is a rare thing, as I believe you know, to find such an unusual person in this town. I don't get out much to meet people, but when I do, I don't normally run into surprises. I'm sure you meet interesting people in St. Louis, but in this grocery store such an occurrence just hadn't happened before. Yet, it had happened. Something told me that this man was an extraordinary person. He completely captured my attention. Finding him was something very rare occurring in life and I sensed it.

But that's beside the point, he was answering my question. I heard him say to me, "I live over at Grantsville with my daughter and her husband. She's a nurse and I'm a carpenter."

At that point, the man pulled out a business card from his inside coat pocket and handed it to me. "I'm handy with wood and building things. Yes, fine lady. I enjoy building things. If you ever need a dresser built or anything, just give me a call." He paused ever so slightly and continued, "Give me a call sometime even if you don't need a dresser built. Another thing I do, I write poetry."

I took the card running my hand over the linen card stock while verifying the man's name. At this point the man winked at the boys who stood totally transfixed. Obviously they, like their mother, had never met such a scintillating, spontaneous person, and I did enjoy poetry.

The man told a few more jokes—ones I found to be truly humorous. And for a moment, right there in the store, the sense of my ordinary world vanished. I felt rejuvenated by the contagious personality of this vivacious fellow. I actually felt drawn to him. He conveyed life, energy. And he was very much a part of the earth, realistic, totally physically alive, uncommon, yet a part of the very air we breathed. Singing and talking, he was more person than I had ever imagined could exist.

In response to his words, I assured him that I would give him a call. I didn't think he really believed me, but I meant it. And at that moment I knew in my mind that I was going to prove to him that I meant it.

Well, still standing there mesmerized by the essence of this man, I continued to press upon my mind to find a reason why I would call him. What he said about dressers had penetrated my consciousness.

While I was mentally working on a list of reasons why I would call this gentleman, he vanished from my sight. Realizing he was sane, I looked down at the business card in my hand. I had his phone number and his address. I tucked the card inside my purse. I did have a project or two in mind, had been thinking about them for a while.

I continued to push my cart ahead finally. I wasn't thinking of my grocery list any longer, although Shane was coaching me and I went down a couple more aisles to get the items I needed. By the time the boys and I had gotten to the check-out stand, I thought about dressers. That was it. The boys needed dressers. I made up my mind at that moment that I'd call Mr. Wellington about some dressers for the boys. I saw how this could work out fine. John had recently mentioned getting two dressers, one for each of the boys. John and I had even gone out looking for some, but the ones we looked at were either too expensive or made to last as long as a cardboard cereal box might last.

So to make sense of all this, Sophie, I finished my shopping that day with a lilt in my step, gathered up the boys and my groceries, rushed out into the drizzling rain packing all into the van. We motored home, arrived in plenty of time for me to fix supper for John. Everything I did seemed elevated. I was even happy about having to get supper. I think you recall how John hates to wait on supper and how I always try to make sure it is ready and hot the very moment he pulls into the driveway. John was, after all, a working man and he needed a good meal at the end of his day. I had always understood this, but I hadn't always been so happy to comply with the demand.

Anyway, soon as we were home, the boys helped carry what they could and we all filed into the house. After I put the groceries away, I punched down the bread dough which was rising on the counter and I took some meat out of the fridge. I told the boys to hang up their wet coats to dry near the furnace and to get out the Legos. I turned on the oven to get some potatoes baking and got the pans out to put some crescent rolls on to rise. I timed everything just so. By my calculations dinner would be ready when John arrived. Of course, my having two ovens was the real thing that would make everything work out.

Now, Sophie, I do have to tell you many more things before I will be satisfied that I've covered the story of my life as it has been since you last heard from me. For instance, I must tell you what happened after getting groceries that day. The whole thing was so typical of how John and I do things. Have I ever said anything that sounds like this? "We're just a happy little family." I'm sure I have made statements like that before. And that is sort of a sad way to describe how the dresser situation worked out.

I was putting the meal together when John pulled up in the driveway. Pork chops were sizzling on the broiler, baked potato aroma filled the kitchen. Corn was cooking and gravy was bubbling on the stove. The timer sounded on the oven above the stove and I rushed over to get the rolls. I took the rolls from the oven and set them on the bread board by the counter.

Right away, in walked John. He was speckled with raindrops. His glasses steamed up like the steam on the window. You should have seen his dark thatch of hair, Sophie. You wouldn't have recognized him. The day before this event, he'd just had it cut short at the barber's. I asked how work was and he gave me the same tired answer he'd given me daily for years.

"Same old, same old," he would reply. And after saying that this night, he went to check on the boys. Then he came back into the kitchen for a cookie.

Everything about that meal has become a freeze in my mind. It will stay with me forever and soon you'll understand why I say that. I hurried over to the rolls with some melted butter to brush onto them.

John stood by the cookie jar fishing out a cookie. I then ran back to the oven to test the potatoes with a fork.

"Potatoes are done," I told John. He ate the cookie as I got out a plate and quickly took the potatoes from the oven. I asked him to place the plate full of potatoes on the table. I enjoyed cooking; I liked the aroma of delectable food at mealtime. I loved to cook, in fact, and I was very glad that John would help put the baked potatoes on the table.

He then picked up a roll and a butter knife and prepared a hot roll to eat. He said to me, "Just testing them to see if they're worth putting on the table." He inhaled half the roll and told me they weren't worth putting on the table. Of course I laughed, played along, wound up the dish towel and gave him a lick on the rear-end.

"What do you mean not fit to eat?" I questioned him. Then I said, "Listen you, stop being a pest and get out of those fancy pants before I have to take them off for you."

John stood licking butter off his thumb. Then raised one eyebrow and told me, "Your cooking is better than anything downtown." He took hold of my arm and pulled me toward him, kissing me with a hint of butter on his lips. And then he asked if I would indeed undress him. Well, he did look good.

Oh, you wish, I thought as we broke away. I would never have told John Olson that! So I wound up the dish towel and gave him another lick on the rear and gave him a nudge toward the hallway. I didn't want the food to get cold. I called for the boys to wash up for supper. They soon entered the kitchen where I inspected their hands and nails. At that moment John returned.

He wore Levi's and a blue sweatshirt. The blue made his eyes stand out even more blue. The scent of his Brute cologne mingled with the aroma of baked potatoes and hot rolls. I furrowed my brows and wrinkled up my nose. He had touched up his cologne and I have to admit that I really didn't care for the smell. It was an unfortunate fact, yet I had never told him. I simply hadn't wanted to upset him.

We all sat down at the table and John said a blessing on the food. But although John looked good, his thoughts, manners and appearance never really fit. That is what I wanted to tell you.

As we sat down to dine, I was dying inside just to tell him about the older gentleman I'd met at the grocery store. I didn't know if it was the right time. One never could know that sort of thing. I sat looking at my baked potato until John stopped eating a moment. And I thought *now I will tell him about the possibility of getting dressers made for the boys. I will tell him right now,* but then he spoke before I got a chance.

"Anne could you pass the butter, please?" he said. "Today the city planners of Salt Lake have decided to build a new park downtown . . ."

I didn't really hear what else John was saying. He went on in his monotone way of speech, seemingly unaware that I was sitting there at the table and that I wanted to tell him something. I really wanted to say something about Mr. Wellington before supper was over. I wanted to be recognized for having some good news to share with my husband. Finally John's eyes circled around the room as he looked at each of us at the table. Silence fell upon us. *I would tell him now,* I thought and began speaking.

"John," I cleared my voice, "Dear, the most interesting thing happened at the grocery store today."

Ben chimed in, "Yes, Dad, you should have been there."

John blinked twice and knitted his brows. "Now Benjamin, your mother is speaking. You'll get a turn." John looked over at me, fluttered his eyelashes as though he were deep in thought. We all paused, waiting, waiting, eyes on John, but no one spoke.

Finally, I continued speaking, nearly stuttering, "There was this older man at the grocery store. He sang a song to us right there in the store. The song was about Tooele water. It was very comical. The boys were totally captivated by him. He could have been an exotic prince from Arabia the way they took to him."

John scratched his ear, his eyebrows pulled together, "So, Anne, who was he?"

I told John that the gentleman lived in Grantsville and that his name was Walter Wellington and as many other things as I could remember of what the man told me. I explained that I really was quite excited about meeting Mr. Wellington.

John sat chewing his food and listening. Suddenly he raised his fork to signal for something. He said, "Anne excuse me a moment. Could you pass the butter please?"

I passed the butter and said, "Anyway, my darling, the reason I remember his name is because he left a business card for me."

John looked up, his eyebrows still knitted, then he said, "So, what does this Mr. Wellington do to warrant possession of a business card?"

I will admit, Sophie, I felt like I as being interrogated. I said to John, "The gentleman builds things. He makes dressers." I finally cut open a potato and surged ahead, "I wondered if we could have him build two dressers for the boys' Christmas? He specifically mentioned dressers."

"That would be great!" Shane interjected. Then there was a pause while everyone sat thinking and passing more food around. I heard Misty, our cat, scratching at the kitchen window.

Finally John looked up from his plate of food, still with knitted brows. "How much does Mr. Wellington charge to make these dressers? And does he make them to last?" He rubbed his hand across his chin.

I told John that I hadn't really asked about a price, but I remembered Mr. Wellington had said that his prices were reasonable. However the exact price? I really didn't know. I continued to plead my cause, "I can call him. Perhaps tomorrow I can call and find out, that is, if we're interested. After all, we have been looking for a sturdy-type of dresser." I struggled very hard to convince John of these facts. I wanted to get the dressers. I wanted to have some real wooden dressers and I thought these were what Mr. Wellington's words promised. I was convinced that he was sincere and that this is what he would provide, no particle boards with stapled ends. I prayed silently for a favorable position from John.

Finally John said, "Sounds sensible. Christmas is coming. You'll need to ask him if he could have them finished in time for Christmas. Then he said, "Speaking of Christmas, we need to choose a family this year for whom to do the Twelve Days of Christmas. So be thinking about it." This tradition is where we take something over to a person's house for twelve days before Christmas.

Sophie, do you know about this tradition? This is a time when we take food or treats anonymously over to a specified person's house. On the first day, we take twelve of something, for example, a dozen hot dinner rolls. The next day, the eleventh day before Christmas we take eleven of something over, cookies, cinnamon rolls or such and so on until the day before Christmas. We usually take one large Christmas cake on that day. I don't know if you recall Mrs. Shields, the widow, but she had been our subject the year before. We try to do it without their knowledge so the neighbor doesn't know who is bringing the treats. It makes for very good neighbors and the boys find it highly satisfying to bring in a spirit of giving and serving others for the holiday season.

With supper over, John sat reading the Deseret News. The boys were bathing and getting ready for bed. John and I talked about Christmas and what we'd be doing.

Now, I've written and written for a long time. In fact the day has passed and the boys should be getting home soon. But, just one more thing while I'm thinking about it and then I'll write more later. I'm feeling a little blue tonight but I'm trying to keep my hands and mind busy. It helps. I'll say for now, I need to think out some things before I can see them more clearly and write more clearly.

Listen, Sophie, I'm sure you've heard me talk of Mrs. Field's Cookies. Well she struck it rich baking up cookies, which is fine with me. I don't need to be rich, just have a little happiness now and again. Some days I wonder if there is life after having a family. When it comes to cooking, cleaning, shopping, planning for the whole family, it can become a chore. Look, you know I mean doing things more along the lines of pursuits in the arts and theater, in learning, in sharing knowledge, or in brushing up on my photography.

I have time to do some of these things yet I seem to be oriented toward pouring all my time and energy into doing for my children, which is fine. The problem is, not once did I think of taking any time out for me. For example, I haven't taken any serious photos since at Yellowstone last summer. I still have that same camera I had in college.

Do you remember that huge campus photo contest they had that one year? I won a blue ribbon. I had taken a photograph of that lake near where we lived. I was someone back then, I had something to offer. I guess what I'm saying is, there was a time when I was liked for who I was as an individual and for what I could do. I was appreciated. I remember those days.

As a matter of fact, remembering things, do you remember I told you of the classes I took in drafting? And how I had wanted to be an architect? I still have that drafting table stored down in the basement. It's gathering dust. I hadn't thought of my drafting table in years. I stumbled on to it the other night looking for something. I'd forgotten I even had one of those. Good grief, can you believe what a sorry fate I've come to?

Somehow, while trying to fulfill my role as wife and mother, I have lost what I could have given to that role. I have been the chief, the maid, the cook, the therapist, the chauffeur, the mat. But, I needed to be the inspiration and the cohesion for my family too. I didn't think we were a dying family. I realize now that I was not seeing the whole sad picture.

One thing I had begun for quite some time was to leave out a crucial part of myself from my endeavors. I had deprived my family circle from the best of me. I'd tied an apron around my waist and a noose around my neck. I would say, "Yes, dear, right away dear," to John and the boys. But, I wasn't being fair to them. I wasn't giving them my best judgment and my best hopes and aspirations. My best taste or highest capabilities wasn't foremost in my thinking. I wasn't inspiring them. I was letting them stay right where they were in their thoughts and dreams. And I wondered about John and me. What had happened to the so called "spiritual marriage" of our two hearts?

I realize that in today's world it is a difficult era for most women like myself. We get mixed signals! We feel like we're supposed to be "Super Moms" and do anything and everything for everybody. Yet inside, we're often running on empty, as they say. I wonder, how are we supposed to fulfill such a role if we haven't developed ourselves? Where are we if we haven't kept our thinking and striving fastened on a broad view and understanding of human potential, of spirituality, of God, of Sainthood, of education, of understanding?

It seems to me that we should never be lost in the details of our work as wives and mothers. We have to aspire to the ends, the goals, our highest aspirations that these roles can fulfill. I believe that my mother taught me to be responsible. But, what I must do is to sit down and relax once in a while on a regular basis and show the boys how to take that same responsibility?

Just as I told you how John always said, "Same old thing. Same old, same old," when I asked of his work for the day. Same old same old is such a sad commentary on John, poor John and the heights to which his dreams could never soar. Poor John believed that same was safe and same was good and that same was happy. Same old, same old! He never allowed himself to dream of anything else. And for a long time perhaps, I didn't either. I also thought that same is safe. Same is good, same is happy. Did I have a dream anymore? But, more of that later.

Same old, same old Sophie. There's so much in that. It's hard NOT be same old, same old, same old. It's so hard, over the years, to continue to explore and to wonder. It's always much easier to say "Same old, same old and thank God for same old, same old."

I wonder if there are any other people out there who have ever had such thoughts as I have? And you Sophie? Have you ever had such thoughts? Have you ever said to yourself, "Same old, same old?" I won't ever let it be same old, same old again! Do you grow weary of anything and everything, of all routines and all chores, of all undertakings that cry out, "Same old, same old?"

I know you will tell me your answer one of these days. In asking the question, I feel a great relief and yet a great fatigue. It takes a lot of energy to ask, "What shall we do?" There will always be same old, same old. But, enough about that for now. I just have one or two other pieces of furniture I have to move before the boys return. I'll write more later.

As ever, Anne

JANUARY 27

Again Sophie I pick up my pen,

The weekend has come and gone and we have had a huge blizzard after the rain on Friday. A big cold front moved through. I feel like an old mountain man holed up for the winter with cabin fever setting in. It would be nice to have the peace and calm of a spring day, a cheery person to talk with, a songbird singing, a lovely cerulean sky and leaves popping out on the sycamore tree.

I dream of all these things because I'm full of feeling and needing to express so many different emotions and so many different problems. I am drained more than you could ever know. So much has happened to me and my losses have been staggering. I'm not able to say, "Oh this past Christmas I received these wonderful toys, these wonderful expressions that have enabled me to entertain myself, to be lighthearted, to be secure?"

No! Instead of that, I must say this Christmas I have received something very much akin to the gifts received by the prophets. The insight into a new dimension of life's experience—my eyes have been opened. My Christmas gift from God in Heaven has been a peeling away of the covers before my eyes. I can see beyond the cave now.

On New Year's Day I made the resolution that I couldn't <u>not</u> think on and on about the significance of the gifts that I received for Christmas. I had to think about my boys. I promised myself that the boys would have my attention. I'm writing all of this to you now and in the puzzling manner by which I have chosen to reveal the facts to you. I do this because I believe all of a piece, but in a continued order, is the way to make the facts the most significant to you as well as to me. And above all, I want to convey the significance of all the experiences I've had. Sometimes I've found myself jotting ideas down on the backs of old envelopes and putting them aside for the moment. I do this mainly because I want to remember what it is that I have to tell you. But I do it especially because I want you to understand my story in the ways in which I choose to reveal it to you for clarity.

In the last words I wrote to you I did say that I had to move the furniture in the living room to rearrange it. That one act on my part turned out to be very good for me. Also, I must mention that I got my hair cut short Saturday. Not Marine short, but shorter than I've ever worn it. You know how John always liked my hair long. Well, I have taken my hairstyle into my own hands and soon you'll understand why I say that. After all, hair grows back!

But, let me go back to November and my having met the old gentleman and afterwards talking about the dressers to John. Well, this morning I found some of my scribbling on the back of a Utah Power envelope. I want to include it now. It's dated November 4:

*Today the sun rays shoot down like golden streamers
in a Macy's Parade. Crisp, clean mountain air sits*

transparent against the blue Oquirrh Mountains; large swatches of pines far away appear deep blue from my kitchen window. Quaking aspens outside my window are quivering in the slight breeze. Marigolds along my walkway have been crushed by killing frosts. Petunias lay dead and brown. I miss the hummingbirds on my front porch, too. The hours of sunlight will soon begin to lengthen at winter solstice, but today I must concentrate on the present hour.

I wrote those words as the sun came up on the morning which I'm trying to remember. The rising sun made me think of my boys and what they were doing that morning, which is to say that this particular morning, the boys decided to go Trick-or-Treating around the neighborhood. They were dressed up as pirates. They were mostly full of notions and dreams of candy treasure, but from time to time they did seem forlorn and lost.

Anyway, glancing at Shane that morning made me think of the time when I was six years old. I was full of dreams, too. I remember long ago, this one day after school; my father took me for a drive in the car to get ice cream. Inside the ice-cream shop, Dad asked which kind of ice cream I wanted. Well, I was more interested in which boy would dip the ice cream for me, the one with the dark hair and glasses or the one with the golden hair. Dad bought me two scoops of ice cream that day, chocolate fudge and butter pecan.

He laughed when we climbed back inside the car. "Anne," he said, "we didn't come across town to choose a boy, we came to get ice cream."

With that I recall quickly eating both flavors but the butter pecan ice-cream cone tasted the best. Of all my memories, I remember how I felt so alone and sad when Daddy died about a month later. But, then that's been over twenty years ago. Now, getting back to the subject in the present moment.

Do you remember my one big dream in college? It was to become a wife and mother. I really didn't take my first year at college seriously. With all of this in mind, I can return to speaking of dreams and November fourth. This particular Saturday, my boys were up early and dressed in the pirate costumes they had worn for Halloween. They raced out of the house without breakfast and charged over to Mrs. Cunningham's next door. I'll bet they were thinking of the glazed donuts and apple cider she gave them on Halloween.

I've always wondered why we celebrate this odd holiday. I don't like ghosts, monsters, goblins, or spiders. Yet these few mentioned are mildly frightening compared to some of the children who come Trick-Or-Treating with fake blood dripping from their mouths, ugly horrific rubber masks, or axes stuck in their heads. I don't relish the skeletons hanging from porches like wind socks either. My boys like to dress up and go around the neighborhood, but in the fun way.

But, back to the point. A few days after Halloween, off loped Ben and Shane like spring colts. They ran to Mrs. Cunningham's and my boys rang her door bell. I heard them proclaim, "Trick-Or-Treat" the moment her front door flew open.

Now for background, let me say that Mrs. Cunningham has been our neighbor for as long as we've lived here, ever since John moved us back to his hometown. Mrs. Cunningham deals with problems in creative ways. Love radiates from her. Although her smile may be a trifle askew, she does radiate goodness and serenity.

To their proclamation, Mrs. Cunningham's bold vibrato voice sliced through the calm morning in reply. "Oh, hello you scary prowlers," she said. "What are you doing out in broad daylight?" Upon hearing this I went outside, closed the door behind me, ran to the old gnarled peach tree, stood behind it out of view to listen to what they were saying.

"We came for treats," the boys answered in unison.

Mrs. Cunningham played along. "My my, I don't know if I should give out treats to pirates. Perhaps I should trick you instead."

I peeked out and saw her zipping up her yellow jacket. Her silver hair was meticulously cut short in back, yet a wave stood tall and wispy in front and on top like fine bird plumage. "Since you're here, could you go around to the back porch? Perhaps Mr. Cunningham could rustle up something for you. I bet you boys are out before breakfast, huh?" The boys heard and responded by running around to the back of the Cunningham's house. At this point I decided I had better go see what the boys were getting into. I strolled over to Mrs. Cunningham's front porch and knocked on the door. Mrs. Cunningham came right out on the steps. She was holding a watering can. I asked what she was planning for my Trick-Or-Treating pirates.

With her brows raised slightly, Mrs. Cunningham said good-naturedly, "Well, pirates need a good breakfast. I'm just frying up some sausages and scrambled eggs with French toast for Mr. Cunningham and I'm sure the boys would enjoy having breakfast with us." She flipped a dry leaf out of the water container she carried, crumpled it and stuck it in her green apron pocket.

I was never surprised by Mrs. Cunningham's hospitality or charm. I had only heard her first name used once or twice all the years we'd lived next door. Her husband had always called her Mrs.

Cunningham and she had always called him Mr. Cunningham. I remember once thinking of them by their first names, Alice and Marcus—but I had never wanted to say them. Anyway, I said to Mrs. Cunningham, "You do like to feed people."

"Yes, yes I do," she answered. "And I have chokecherry syrup." She took hold of my hand and patted it, "Why don't you tell your Johnny to come over too and the six of us will have breakfast together."

Mrs. Cunningham stood slightly shorter than I, yet her shoulders were squared and she stood regally erect. She stepped out to the sidewalk and snapped several frozen marigold blooms off and put them in her jacket pocket.

"Oh, how I do miss the gorgeous flowers of summer," I said, "and I'm longing for those sun-filled days."

Mrs. Cunningham nodded in agreement then began humming a lilting tune.

I have to tell you Sophie, never have I heard Mrs. Cunningham say anything bad about another human being. In the years I've know her, she has been a fine example of how folks should treat other folks. However, she has always had plenty to say regarding bad neighborhood dogs. She knows all the dogs on the block by name. Sometimes I have heard her shouting out warnings to them. You would die laughing to hear her once she gets going. She simply will not tolerate bad dogs. She has a little collie named Shasta and she won't allow Shasta to be bullied by what she calls "those mongrel hellions."

Truly she has been and is so good-natured. She makes people happy. I know that when she asked if we would eat over, I felt excited, thrilled to have such a caring neighbor. "I'll go get John," I told her and I gave her a squeeze around her shoulders as she stood up from plucking more dead marigold heads.

Her pale blue-green eyes pierced right through me as she fastened her gaze on me. The muscles in her face were pulled up into a smile. She said, "Run along now. I've got pirates at my back door." She pointed a slender finger toward my house as a signal to get me going. "And hurry back. I'll have hot cocoa ready when you return."

I still marvel at the neighborliness of most the people here in the area. Being raised outside of Chicago, I didn't realize while growing up that there was such a thing as a "neighbor." We had family members and each other, but we didn't really talk to anyone who lived inside the houses along our street. But in Tooele, I know all the neighbors up and down our street. Really, people here are friendly and giving. My neighbors seem to be the embodiment of "good will toward men" that I hear so often quoted only at Christmas time.

And I like the landscape. I enjoy the rhythmic heartbeat of the country and the crisp clean days of simply looking out across the valley. Listen, Sophie, I never tire of the scent of sagebrush following a rain storm. In fact I adore this place in the foothills. There are no high rises, no condominiums, no L-trains, no homeless people, very few cynics. It truly is a grand place in my estimation. I feel warm and safe inside because this town has become my town too.

Regardless, that morning in November, I went over to tell John about the breakfast invitation. He acted put out by the invitation as if I had been gullible to accept Mrs. Cunningham's offer. I couldn't comprehend his reaction so I ignored it and he certainly did come along with me. After all, John enjoys good food as much as anyone ever could and he knew that Mrs. Cunningham could cook delicious food.

Well, we walked over and knocked at the front door. Mr. Cunningham let us in and I could see the boys were enjoying some hot cocoa all ready and being entertained by some of Mrs. Cunningham's stories of her dog, Shasta.

John and I stepped inside and the aroma of sausage cooking and hot cocoa filled the air. I felt hungry inside. Of course, tall Mr. Cunningham led us right into the kitchen and we sat down at the long maple table. It was adorned with sunflower place mats. A dollop of whipped cream set off each cup of steaming cocoa. Mr. Cunningham offered a blessing on the food and we visited as we ate. I have to admit, the food was absolutely delicious which is always true at Mrs. Cunningham's house whether it is breakfast, lunch, or supper.

The boys had excused themselves so Mrs. Cunningham and I could visit. And Mr. Cunningham had meandered out into the garage to show John and the boys some of the little clocks he was building. Little indeed! Why, in fact, he makes grandfather clocks sometimes. They are fabulous. He crafted the one that stands inside our house.

Well, with John and the boys out of the room, we two women had a moment to get to some heartfelt issues. First we began talking about upcoming Thanksgiving events. I took the opportunity to tell her that my side of the family was coming this year since John's family were nearby and always had a huge gathering at Uncle Jake's house. But I was really dying to talk about Steve, my brother. I'm sure you remember Sophie, the one time at college when he came to see me? Steve Ross, what a kidder and pest at times. No one could forget Steve. Anyway, to continue, I asked Mrs. Cunningham if she remembered Steve.

"Oh course," she said, "and what a ham bone he is, always trying to get a rise out of anyone who comes along."

And, when she said that, I got all wistful and weepy. I told Mrs. Cunningham all about Steve's last assignment in Nicaragua and in Bolivia and about his work in army intelligences. Do you remember the note about it? Well, even though I talk to Mrs. Cunningham nearly every day, I hadn't told her about our misfortune. So I took that moment to tell her how we believed that Steve had been murdered down there.

Remember, Sophie, I told you that it had been several months before we even found out where he was stationed and where he had gone. We wanted to believe that he might one day come back, but we didn't have any tangible hope that that could be the case.

Mrs. Cunningham was sympathetic of course. She said, "Oh, Anne, I didn't know about that. I'm so sorry." Her collie ran up and jumped onto her lap. She said, "You good doggie. Are those mean mutts in town terrorizing you again? She fussed a moment and then turned her complete attention back to thoughts about Steve. "You didn't tell me about his funeral."

"Actually we never had a funeral for him," I said, "We'd hoped his death was a rumor. We really didn't know what had happened to him and we simply hadn't received any information for such a long time." I went on to explain to her that the army had set a death date. There was no body, no real explanation, merely a "We regret to inform you that your son is missing following intelligence work." That type of letter.

Sophie, you know how much I missed Steve. He was my only brother. Just the idea that I couldn't talk to him by phone or write to him bothered me very much. I missed his silly jokes and I told Mrs. Cunningham all that while we sat talking.

It was a very impactful experience. I had the opportunity talking with Mrs. Cunningham, to tell her about the many times John and Steve would go hunting deer and rabbits together when we were first married. They'd go hunting whenever Steve came up. I know that John had become bitter inside, after the news about Steve, or rather the non-news, the uncertainty and then finally the army's decision to declare him dead and gone. John, as a matter of fact became very distant after that news. It was as if something was eating away at him. Steve was one of the few outlets for expression and camaraderie that poor John had ever had. It was sad to think about this fact, but it was helpful for me to remember the good times about my brother Steve and to share some of these with Mrs. Cunningham.

Mrs. Cunningham was petting Shasta as she listened. She asked me, "What kind of things did you young people do growing up near Chicago? She gave a hopeful smile. That smile brought back one particular memory to me.

I remembered that back in Illinois as a young girl, and after my father had died, my mother would sometimes go out with men who seemed to swarm to our house like ants to a sugar cube. One particular time when I was eleven and Steve was thirteen, there was some construction going on down the block of some big fine apartment buildings. We children enjoyed strolling down the street to watch the bustle of buildings being constructed right before our eyes.

The workers would all drive up in their trucks and cars to the location where they were building. Then they'd spend all day working. But everything would stop about noon and a hush would fall upon the whole area. You could almost hear men eating their sandwiches. It was summer time so we didn't have to go to school.

Well, this one day we were out on the porch, eating popcorn and drinking lemonade, just passing time on a hot summer day. All of a sudden these two bronzed workers walked up to our house. They were asking for directions, and the address they wanted was ours. Steve and I just looked at each other. Steve asked the workers if they lived in town.

The men didn't, so Steve told them they had the wrong street, that it was two blocks over going north or something. Anyway he gave them misguided directions.

The taller man acted puzzled and scratched his head. He was much taller than Mother, and handsome, with big muscles. But we wondered why he had our address. "Who are you looking for?" Steve asked them finally.

They said in unison, "We're looking for a woman named Abby Ross. Do you know her?" "Is this where she lives?"

Of course, Steve nearly choked on his popcorn. He wasn't about to have our mother swooped down on by these out-of-town workers. About that time Mother opened the door and stepped outside on the porch to ask us if we needed more lemonade. She hadn't heard the conversation and she hadn't seen the men. One of the men whistled and Mother looked up and flashed her dark eyes at them congenially. The men were leaning on our porch staring at her as soon as they noticed our mother, but they didn't know she was Abby Ross.

That's when Steven yelled, "Yellow Jacket!" as if he'd been stung. He threw his syrupy lemonade right on the man's head, the one who'd asked about Abby Ross. With Steve's quick motion, he upset the bowl full of popcorn and it went flying right onto those two workers. Some of the popcorn stuck to the lemonade that had already stuck to their clothes. They both huffed off looking a little miffed.

I don't think they ever came back, which is understandable. If they realized the address was correct, I'm sure that Steve's actions had scared them off for good. That was a great summer. And as I said, when we were children we had few worries, but now as an adult there are constantly major decisions to make. And there as I sat talking to Mrs. Cunningham, I felt like she understood me without my having to pretend to be grown up.

And Sophie, when I told Mrs. Cunningham about Steve, her head was bobbing right along with the story while she listened. Shasta was as attentive as Mrs. Cunningham. "My, that was quite the adventure," she said. "I can see why you would miss a character like that."

I remember thinking when she said this, *yes I certainly do*. And about that time I asked if I could have a glass of water. But suddenly Shasta jumped up and began barking. She bolted out of the room and took off outside, barking even more. Mrs. Cunningham sprinted to the door moving as deftly as Shasta. And right then and there she started in, "Oh dammit! There's those two mongrel Australian shepherds again." Mrs. Cunningham ran back to the kitchen and returned wielding a broom. "Damn there dirty hides," she muttered. Then she hurled herself out the door and dashed off at a fast clip. I could see there was going to be a showdown. I jumped up and ran to the door to see what would happen.

Mrs. Cunningham sprinted halfway down the block after the dogs swearing at them, "You little bleep-itty-bleep-bleeps stay out of my yard. And don't you come back you ragged hellions!" Since they were out of range for swatting, she picked up a rock and flung it at them. Her aim struck its mark and the smaller dog yelped off into a side yard. "And don't you come back!" she yelled.

While she was walking back to the house, I got a drink of water, stood there sipping the water and wondered why I couldn't be expressive of my feelings like this woman was. I regretted that I lacked stamina and grit.

When Mrs. Cunningham returned to the house she capered back inside. She looked in the mirror, carefully arranged her hair, and stepped back into the kitchen. I don't think she realized it, but those little mongrels kept her in pretty athletic condition for a woman of nearly eighty.

As though nothing had even transpired, Mrs. Cunningham calmly invited me to sit down with my cup of water. It hadn't been the first time she'd followed this format. She crossed her legs at the ankle and sat comfortably at the kitchen table and continued the conversation. "I hope you like the water. It's the best water in these parts." She arranged her wispy hair one more time and said, "Why don't we check on those boys of ours." She carefully rose to her full stature and gracefully led the way toward the garage. I followed her.

The boys stood listening intently to Mr. Cunningham tell about the history of a clock he was working on. John was leaning up against a shelf nearby nodding his head. The organized garage had room for one car and a whole array of odd tools and equipment that Mr. Cunningham worked with during the days. He also liked to carve things out of willows. He had taught the boys how to make willow whistles, sling shots, and stick horses too.

Mr. Cunningham looked up as we entered the area and nodded while greeting us congenially. We all visited a while then John mentioned that we had a few chores to complete back home like raking up the rest of the leaves in the yard.

Oh it was a wonderful day. I enjoyed visiting with Mrs. Cunningham. It had done me a world of good. As I had told the Cunningham's earlier, my mother would be coming to dinner at my house for Thanksgiving and then she'd be staying a couple of weeks to complete Christmas shopping and maybe even stay for Christmas. I had plenty to get accomplished before Thanksgiving. And of course, I hoped to get hold of Mr. Walter Wellington soon to see if he could make some dressers for me.

Before winding this up for the time, Sophie, I have a question for you. It has to do with Halloween. Didn't you tell me that it is really a Catholic holiday? All Hallows Eve? That November first is All Saints Day. And November second is All Soul's Day? You pray for the saints living and dead? How did we get a negative idea of witches and terrifying ghosts? Is that what the Protestant Reformation has come up with? And the American way of life and all the silly unhistorical theories we have? I want you to know that on November first, I thought of you and I prayed for the saints I know about in the New Testament, Luke, James, John, Paul, and Timothy. We believe we are saints too in the latter days. I have only been a Latter-day Saint for six years. Do you refer to yourself as a saint or just a regular person? I don't recall exactly what you told me.

I enjoy the stories of St. Teresa. I remember when I was visiting you two years ago, and you had the sisters give me some St. Albert's water for Ben; he had been so sick with a fever. You told me that the sisters at the monastery would pray daily for him. I still have that little bottle. It's empty now. I do believe in prayer and healing. I put the holy water on Ben's forehead every day for two weeks and he recovered totally. The more prayers the better! I had the Latter-day Saints praying for him and the Catholic sisters too. It was very consoling. I know that prayer does achieve miracles.

Why don't you call me sometime? You have my phone number. I've tried to get through to you several times, but I either get your message service or a receptionist that seems uninformed . . . Does she know who you are? Maybe she hasn't been there long. Oh, Sophie, some days, I can see very clearly how I wanted to develop in my life, to change, to be every day a better person, to always be a sincere dreamer. Thinking of being a dreamer makes me think of a book I read recently.

I've been reading <u>Real Moments</u> by Barbara De Angelis. It has given me many new insights. She points out in one part about simply taking three minutes, three times a day for those people in your life who are usually neglected. For example: wise teachers and spiritual counselors such as you, Sophie, or husbands, and children. You could add anyone you want to the list.

Well, I've got big dreams, my dear lady, and I've realized they're going to come true now, because I'm going to work on them. You're the one who planted the notion of "doing something about dreams" in my head and I thank you so much. I can hear you saying, "Anne, you've got to think on a grander scale! Forget nickels and dimes! The world is waiting for you." I remember in college how we had dreams, I wanted to be a wife and mother, as well as being a photographer and a draftsman.

If anyone found out my other dream they'd think I wasn't sane. Do you remember? Yes, you do remember. A cowboy! I'm not into the politically correct cowgirl stuff. I just want to be a cowboy. If I dressed in Levi's and cowboy boots around here, I'm sure people would wonder what I was up to. There are lots of folks here that are cowboys and proud of it. I must have been a cowboy in the pre-existence, in the world where we lived before being born to earth. I probably had a grand horse ranch too. And you may have been my guide and guardian there, too. I don't remember, do you?

Much love,

Anne

P.S. Recently I've been reading *The Eve of St. Agnes* which is a poem by John Keats. I just wanted to include a few lines here that I was reading.

I

St. Agnes Eve - Ah bitter chill it was!
The owl, for all his feathers, was a-cold;
The hare limped trembling through the frozen grass,
And silent was the flock in woolly fold:
Numb were the Beadsman's fingers while he told
His rosary, and while his frosted breath,
Like pious incense from a censor old,
Seemed taking flight for heaven, without a death,
Past the sweet Virgin's picture, while his prayer he saith.

V

At length burst in the argent revelry,
With plume, tiara, and all rich array,
Numerous as shadows haunting faerily

The brain new-stuffed, in youth, with triumphs gay
Of old romance. These let us wish away,
And turn, sole-thoughted, to one Lady there,
Whose heart had brooded, all that wintry day,
On love, and winged St. Agnes' saintly care,
As she had heard old dames full many times declare.

VI

They told her how, upon St. Agnes' Eve,
Young virgins might have visions of delight,
And soft adornings from their loves receive,
Upon the honeyed middle of the night,
If ceremonies due they did aright:
As, supperless to bed they must retire,
And couch supine their beauties, lily white:
Nor look behind, nor sideways, but require
Of Heaven with upward eyes for all that they desire.

VII

Full of this whim was thoughtful Madeline:
The music, yearning like a god in pain,
She scarcely heard: her maiden eyes divine,
Fixed on the floor, saw many a sweeping train
Pass by - she heeded not at all: in vain
Came many a tiptoe, amorous cavalier,
And back retired; not cooled by high disdain,
But she saw not: her heart was otherwhere:
She sighed for Agnes' dreams, the sweetest of the year.

VIII

She danced along with vague, regardless eyes,
Anxious her lips, her breathing quick and short:
The hallowed hour was near at hand: she sighs
Amid the timbrels, and the thronged resort
Of whisperers in anger, or in sport:
'Mid looks of love, defiance, hate, and scorn,
Hoodwinked with faery fancy; all amort,
Save to St. Agnes and her lambs unshorn,
And all the bliss to be before tomorrow morn.

IX

So, purposing each moment to retire,
She lingered still. Meantime, across the moors,
Had come young Porphyro, with heart on fire
For Madeline. Beside the portal doors,
Buttressed from moonlight, stands he, and implores
All saints to give him sight of Madeline,
But for one moment in the tedious hours,
That he might gaze and worship all unseen:
Perchance speak, kneel, touch, kiss - in sooth such
things have been.

X

He ventures in: let no buzzed whisper tell:
All eyes be muffled, or a hundred swords
Will storm his heart, Love's fev'rous citadel:
For him, those chambers held barbarian hordes,
Hyena foemen, and hot-blooded lords,

Whose very dogs would execrations howl
Against his lineage: not one breast affords
Him any mercy, in that mansion foul,
Save one old beldame, weak in body and in soul.

XI

Ah, happy chance! The aged creature came,
Shuffling along with ivory-headed wand,
To where he stood, hid from the torch's flame,
Behind a broad hall-pillar, far beyond
The sound of merriment and chorus bland:
He startled her; but soon she knew his face,
And grasped his fingers in her palsied hand,
Saying, "Mercy, Porphyro! Hie thee from this place:
They are all here tonight, the whole blood-thirsty
race!"

Sophie, that's all I have time to write for the moment. More later.

Anne

TUESDAY FEBRUARY 13

Dear Sophie,

It is now February thirteenth. I've been away from my task of writing you for several days now, about a week, I guess. And even today I may have to cut my writing short. The furnace broke in the middle of last night and quite truthfully we nearly froze to death. I had to call up the repairman and he said that, hopefully, he could come over this afternoon. Well, until he arrives I shall try to write.

I had called Mrs. Cunningham first thing this morning to see if we could come over to her house until we got the furnace going again. She said "Yes," naturally. Shane was in school, I took Ben over to her house and now I'm sitting at her kitchen table writing to you. Mr. Cunningham has some meeting to attend this morning or he and Ben would be working on some project. As it is, Ben is busy looking at books of animals and he is happy to be in this much warmer place.

I don't know if I mentioned that John's parents have been out of town for vacation this week. They felt like they absolutely needed to get away for a while and pretty soon you'll understand more about that. In the mean time I do miss them since being faced with this attack of cold weather. I feel quiet fretful with all the things I have to concern myself with. Mrs. Cunningham is a godsend and I'm very grateful for her.

On my way over, I picked up a few notes that I had written down with November dates. I planned to include those comments in this writing. As soon as I arrived here around 9:15 a.m., Mrs. Cunningham had some steaming spiced apple cider for us to sip. I never was able to finish telling you about Walter Wellington. First let me set the mood of Thanksgiving, which relates to the story of Mr. Wellington. I'll insert a little writing which I have here on the back of a telephone bill dated November 16:

> *I stood outside on the porch this morning. With deer and elk hunting season nearly over, the hills and fields are clad in ocher hues. The grain fields are reduced to brown stubble or turned into the soil to rest till spring planting. Another gray overcast day; gray with a few snowbirds winging from tree to tree looking, searching for seeds. Ah well, I tell myself, a great day for reading and thinking. Even though I enjoy the distinct changing of each season, I wonder when the first snow will arrive to blanket the earth. And when will spring sunshine thaw the cold dormant soil?*
>
> *I look forward to watching the spring plowing, planting; Buds on trees popping open, and green! Green leafing into summer with the pendulum of life in full swing. Lazy azure-sky-days of summer and the sycamore*

stretching higher and wider and never last long enough for me. I can nearly smell summer - summer sunshine like electricity, hot and vibrant; yet, here it is only autumn.

Well, that is my way. Thinking of the seasons makes me gasp at the rapid change that occurs from spring to summer, to fall, to winter; Seasons that flow on and on, onward without fail, like a giant river. The ebbing and flowing keep the seasons pulsating along, but here it is autumn. Autumn fog hangs on the mountain peaks making the jagged rocks appear much like bearded sentinels guarding the valley.

Winter will pelt the walkways of town with ice and snow and oh my, Christmas. And, the thought of Christmas coming...Right now it's autumn. I should be thinking about Walter Wellington and those wooden dressers, those wooden chests of drawers that he might be able to make. I would really like to think of that. That very day in November, as soon as I could, I stopped what I was doing and I found the card with Mr. Wellington's phone number. I called him. He sounded surprised to discover I was calling him.

"Didn't think I'd hear from you," he said, "but come over to my house. Yes my fine young lady, I'll show you things I've built. It'll help you get an idea of what kind of work I do."

Happy, happy words! In fact, they thrilled me. I was standing there by the phone saying to myself, *there you are, you're making a decision. See you can do it.* After all, I reminded myself that although John had kindly agreed, I said to myself in self-satisfaction; *You, Anne, were the one who initiated and carried through on this project.*

I was and remain very pleased with myself. I was looking to buy two fine solid wood dressers, well-made and to purchase them for a hundred dollars each. It was a deal beyond my dreams. It was wonderful.

It also proved that I could carry out an idea. It proved that I was going make the most out of life, that I was going to do the right thing and successfully so. I was very excited with my newfound self-realization.

The very next day I drove over to this gentleman's house. No trouble getting there. It was on a familiar old road and made an impressive picture looking east toward the mountains. Tall poplar trees framed the grand old house. I realized it was the old Bevan place and it was being kept up quite well, nothing absolutely gone to weed and the driveway neatly trimmed of weeds, with the grounds overall in very good upkeep. After I parked, I went up to the house and rang the doorbell. I was soon ushered inside by the son-in-law, Nels Johnson.

Mr. Wellington was in the kitchen cooking. As soon as he caught sight of me, he stopped his cooking momentarily and greeted me in a happy fashion. He gave me a wide grin. "I'll be right with you," he called standing in front of the kitchen range. He told me that he liked to cook.

What a character the old man was. He wore a white chef's apron. He pulled it straighter, washed his hands in the kitchen sink and came over to where I was standing in the hall.

"I'm glad you stopped by," he told me. "Let me show you some of my work. You can get an idea whether you would like to have something I've made." He looked around. "See this stair railing and banister? I made it." He began pointing things out to me as he continued to talk. Finally, he pointed out a rocking chair in the corner of one room, telling me that he had made it.

I moved over to look more closely at the chair, then, I moved back to the banister and ran my hand over the smooth sanded surface. "Oh these are all very nicely done and beautifully finished." Yes, I was very impressed.

He led me ahead to another room "Look, here is my daughter's work room. Yes, my good lady, I made this table, this lamp base and that little cabinet you see there over against that wall. And I made them to last, to last a long time. And I just finished this dresser." With that he pulled out an empty drawer and showed me the runners and how they worked.

"Just a little bar of soap over the edge now and again, maybe as often as once a year and that's all it takes - keeps it running. Listen, I'll tell you one thing, when I make a dresser, it's the only one YOU'LL ever need if you live as long as Methuselah and your children too. No matter how old they get, I tell you, I build them to last a long time." He gave me a wink.

Charming, that's what he was. And to my eye, he was good. A very fine person indeed, satisfied with his work and happy with himself. I told him my thoughts about him.

He blushed. "Look, let me check on the steaks and I'll take you out to my shop and show you some more things. I'll be right back."

I caught the intense aroma of steaks frying. It made my stomach growl. And standing in the doorway made me think of when I was a few years old. I remembered my dad standing in our old door frame at our house there in Illinois. I heard him come in and I ran to him. He said, "Anne, how would you like a good sirloin steak?" I could always expect a delicious meal when Daddy was doing the cooking.

But back in the present, I felt at home with this engaging spry grandfatherly fellow. He certainly looked vivacious and at that moment I wondered how old he was.

When he returned he said, "I took the meat off the stove. Now where were we?" I listened to Mr. Wellington as he pointed out more items of handiwork. He didn't exactly tell me how old he was, but he said he was doing this work before his dear wife died. She had died nearly thirty years ago. He continued, ". . . and I'm still doing this work today." As he talked on, telling me many other things that were interesting, he led the way outside to his shop. The sun shone through the cerulean sky that day with not one cloud visible on the horizon.

Once we entered his shop, he pulled out an old dusty book of his poetry, took it off a high shelf and began to read the poems aloud. A tear came to my eyes as he read one about his wife leaving this world for a better one. Mr. Wellington had to be one of the last of the all-time fine fellows. Perhaps this was only an impression, but it was my impression and it was positive. He didn't seem to have any common flaws that are so visible in so many people today, in either character or personality. I wondered right then and there why he'd never remarried.

He told me of the time he'd been getting some building materials in his old 64 Chevy pickup. "I was just driving along trying to get through some traffic and my window was rolled down. A young fellow behind me thought I was traveling too slowly. So when I pulled to a stop at my destination, he ran up, and broke out my side window with a rock. He grabbed me around the neck and nearly choked me to death. I wouldn't have believed such a thing was possible, but, he broke my collar bone and it took me a while to recover." He adjusted his wire-framed spectacles and looked more serious than before.

"I don't mess around anymore with tough guys. Since then, I carry a Billy club right on the seat in my truck. One time after that, a guy wanted to come through my open window. I clubbed his hands with that little stick and he backed right off. A lot of these young fellows see me and must think that I'm just an old man, an easy mark who can't defend myself. I've learned to use my head and this Billy club."

"In Salt Lake?" I asked.

"Oh yes, right over near Midvale. Just because my hair is silver doesn't mean I can't think any more."

Listen, Sophie, I know people can be cruel. We see it on TV all the time. Like that guy chasing me in the car a week ago. We live in America, land of the free! Free to kill, hurt, maim, and be idiots if we want! But, is that true freedom? I'm not sure that's what the founders of the nation intended. We have the freedom to be as stupid as we choose. I simply can't understand why other human beings would choose to be so brutal, so uncaring, so insensitive. Where has the love of humanity gone? Was it Wordsworth or Coleridge who bemoaned man's inhumanity to man. And that was back in the nineteenth century and here we are almost at the end of the twentieth century and I'm bemoaning the same thing. But to return to our discussion about Mr. Wellington, he was truly a man in touch with reality.

I had asked Mr. Wellington then and there, "How would you like to build a couple of good-sized dressers for my two boys?"

"Well, how big?" he said in a peppy manner while squinting through his spectacles.

"I'll talk to my husband, John, to find out how large they should be. But, I imagine each will need to be at least four feet high or a little taller with five or six drawers and a smaller drawer at the top. And maybe the drawers should be three and a half feet across." I used my hands to demonstrate the approximate dimensions.

I could see the wheels in Mr. Wellington's mind start to spin. He was calculating in his head. "Yes indeed. The sooner I get the measurements, the less I'll have to work on Christmas Eve. You get them to me soon as possible."

When he said this, I took a deep breath, bit my lip in contemplation of what I told him. What if my estimates were not correct? I wondered if John would agree, but then again, John had left it up to me, so I wasn't going to worry inordinately about it. The next thing that occurred to me was to make some gesture to Mr. Wellington. "What are you planning on doing for Thanksgiving day?" I asked him.

"Well let's see," he replied, "sometimes I just cook dinner for the three of us. This year, I'll be spending the day alone since my daughter and son-in-law are both going elsewhere for Thanksgiving." He rubbed his eyes and adjusted his spectacles. Then he said, "I have a grandson down in Dallas who comes up to putter around with me when he has a chance to get up in this part of the country." He cocked his eyebrows. "I pretty much raised him. Yes indeed I did."

I didn't really hear his last comments because I was thinking how lonely it must be to cook dinner alone on Thanksgiving and then have no one there to eat with you. An idea popped into my head. I blurted out, "Why don't you come to our house for Thanksgiving?" He looked at me and then he gazed toward the mountains a minute.

I went on, "We're having about twenty family members over. We'd enjoy having you as our guest. One or two certainly would make the party more lively."

He delayed his answer as though he were weighing some matters in his mind. His hand went to his chin as if to help him think better. He still didn't answer.

"Well, I don't want to put any pressure on you. We'd be more than happy to have you over to our house. But of course, I won't be offended if you can't make it. Why don't you think about it and let me know later," I said. After that there was a slight pause.

He walked over to the back gate and motioned for me to look at one more item that he had made. "I designed and built this little fireplace," he told me. "I built it this summer so we could cook outdoors."

I looked closely at the structure. It was made of local cobblestones and not overly big. It was very pleasing to behold. "Oh, it is very lovely," I said. I raked my hands through my hair hoping every strand was in place. I'd been so excited about looking at the dressers that I couldn't remember if I'd even combed my hair before leaving the house. "Well, I better get home," I told him. "I enjoyed seeing your marvelous woodwork. What a great ability you have to make plain pieces of wood come to life."

Hearing this compliment from me, his hands went into the pockets of his overalls.

I continued talking, "I appreciate your showing me these fine items that you have made and I hope to be in contact with you soon. I left my boys with a neighbor and I need to be getting home for them."

He thanked me for stopping by. "It was a pleasure to talk to you," he said. "Yes, indeed it was." He rubbed his hand across his forehead.

Then he watched to make sure I backed safely out of the driveway. He waved at me and turned back toward the house. I waited a moment and saw him disappear inside the house. Then I accelerated away and motored home.

I feel, Sophie, that I learned several commendable things about Mr. Wellington that particular day and during that brief visit. For example, he cooked for the three that were in this household, his son-in-law, daughter, and himself. His daughter worked twelve hour shifts as a nurse and so she was never home long enough to do much around the house. The house at Grantsville wasn't his own home, but it was a place to call home for the time being. It was a living arrangement, better than an apartment and homier than a mansion. But best of all, he could live with part of his own family.

But, anyway, Thanksgiving was right around the bend and I needed to think about getting ready for company. And so Thanksgiving Day came. It arrived crisp and cold in the valley. Fog hung low along the base of the mountains, obscuring the canyons. Mother came down from Idaho two days prior to the big event to avoid the big traffic rush on Wednesday. My oldest sister, Kathy, who lives near Denver, arrived with her eight children. These children had mostly grown into men and women, all pretty much teenagers or older.

Kathy's husband, Robert, was able to come this year with her. I guess Robert had told the firm that he refused to work on Thanksgiving and he felt that they would survive without him for a day or two. I was proud of my brother-in-law. He wasn't taking the nonsense these days from his boss who drove all his employees as if he thought they were mules. I was proud of Robert for standing up to the brass.

Anyway, they arrived late in the night and thus everything was in disarray. Having late-night visitors made me think once again of my brother Steven. When we were teenagers, I never knew what he was up to. Late night adventure could have been his middle name.

Well, speaking of Steve at this point in life, at the time of that Thanksgiving, I felt angry inside because I really missed him. I missed the masculine smell of his English Leather cologne, his lilting voice, and his zest for engaging times. I was angry at him. When I looked in the mirror that morning I said to my reflection, "Why did he have to go into intelligence work for the army?" I was thinking how unfair it all was that his life seemingly had been cut short. He'd disappeared from my life. A lump rose in my throat and I didn't want to think about it anymore. After all, Thanksgiving was a day of celebration and prayerful gratitude. It was not supposed to be a bitter day.

My other sister, JoEllen, and her husband Nick, the ones who live in Salt Lake City, drove up in time for dinner at 1:00 p.m. They brought their three daughters.

Well, Sophie, I don't know if you ever cook dinner for your students, but I have to tell you, I got up at 5:30 a.m. in order to get an early start at putting the turkey on to cook. I wanted plenty of time to cook the turkey thoroughly. After putting the turkey in the oven, I checked on my sleeping boys and then went back to bed. As I drifted into slumber, I had an interesting dream.

In my dream it was springtime. There were apple blossoms loading the branches of the several trees surrounding a meadow. I saw two people riding horses through the green pasture. The riders were a man and a woman and they seemed to be intimately joined in conversation. They soon stopped beside a clear pool and dismounted beside an apple in full bloom. The gentleman helped the woman from her horse and caught her up into his arms. He threw off his hat and tossed it to the ground. She unloosed her bonnet and did likewise.

I didn't know who the golden-haired gentleman was, but I realized that the woman in my dream was me. I was surprised that this stranger was holding me. He kissed me on my lips and then on my neck. A tingle of excitement filled my heart and mind. My pulse raced. It was like a sweet sacrament, our souls melding together at that moment. I had no idea who this man was, but I would not soon forget the way he made me feel in my dream. It seemed odd that I would entertain such a dream as this.

But I know something about this dream. It sprang from thoughts of All Hallow's Eve—Halloween. Once you taught me about a big adjustment over Halloween, American style. Yes, Halloween, I studied the subject, including reading and learning Keats' poem, *The Eve of St. Agnes*. What a beautiful thought that poem conveyed. That on All Hallow's Eve, maidens would dream of their future husband.

When I rose an hour later to baste the turkey, I felt silence enwrap me. I heard the hum from the refrigerator while the electric clock above the sink ticked softly. Of course, I welcomed these moments of silence, because they are always healing moments to my soul. During a power outage is one of my favorite times of contemplation, a euphoric experience for me. I feel in total connection with myself and my universe during these moments of raw silence with no electric item humming.

But I was thinking that on Thanksgiving morning, after the silence, it was inevitable that total chaos would be unleashed: showers, hair blowers, CD jazz, timers ticking, and John would be bringing out his banjo to whip up a fast rendition of anything that would suit his fancy. John was usually a quiet man and a man so self-contained and understated that I often wondered what he might be thinking or doing—but at Thanksgiving he could be as noisy as the others. I couldn't criticize John because I did depend on him. He was my security and I knew it. I never wanted to boss him—but there were times I felt so isolated, so isolated.

John was dutiful and helpful. That morning for instance, just as soon as John showered, he had asked what needed to be done and how he might help me. After that he went to the garage and brought in two long tables. We set them up in the dining room overlapping them into the kitchen. The part of the table that was in the kitchen would be occupied by the younger children. That was especially necessary in case of spills. I didn't want to worry about a soiled carpet on Thanksgiving Day.

And of course, Sophie, the day had just started. While preparing things for Thanksgiving, John's mood seemed improved. He was joking and laughing and even gave me a hug.

"You're a nice girl Anne," he said.

And I replied, "Oh, well, I wonder how long you've thought that?"

"About as long as I've known you," he said. "The first time I met you at college, I thought you were nice enough."

"You don't say. Well, it's a very good thing that you did, because now, we're just an old married couple," I told him that day.

Thinking of my dream does bring a smile to me. And I'm sharing it with you for so many reasons. Soon it will be clear to you.

Anyway as we were preparing things, John raised his eyebrows. "I guess Mr. Wellington isn't coming for dinner?" he said since Mr. Wellington hadn't called.

"What? Oh, I guess not," I said. "He never did call. Maybe he had other plans."

"Well, I'd like to meet him. He sounds like a crazy old fellow. I just wonder what it is about him you find so charming."

I blushed, "Maybe you'll never find out," I told him. John was such a solemn, serious man. One couldn't put too much emphasis into praising another. "Now John, get those nimble fingers of yours flying around that bread Maestro. Pretend you're plucking the strings of your banjo." I went to the closet to get a lace tablecloth out and then brought out the stoneware and silverware.

John got glasses from the cupboard. "Here, let me help you prepare for the wining and dining of our guests." He set the glasses on the counter and helped straighten the tablecloth.

I stepped into the living room and turned on a Mozart selection. It helped put a bounce in my step. Back in the kitchen, I saw that John had turned his gaze on me. He was knitting his brow, "Are your relatives ever going to get out of bed?" he asked me. He continued putting the glasses in a row at the table.

I said, "I hope so. I need some more help in the kitchen." I felt like wringing my hands because I wasn't getting everything accomplished when it needed to be done. I asked him, "Could you break the bread up for the dressing?" with that said, I started downstairs.

Suddenly the phone rang. I answered. It turned out to be Mr. Wellington.

"I hate to call you so late on Thanksgiving Day," he said, "yes I do, but I wondered if I could come for dinner after all."

"Oh yes, that would be splendid. Do come as soon as you can. We'd be delighted to have you over," I answered.

"My grandson turned up on my door step yesterday," he added. "We've been building a few things together. And I was just going to cook dinner for the two of us but, last night, late, I mentioned that I'd been invited for dinner. He wondered if he could come along. He's just a young thing, and I thought it might do him good to be around a family setting for Thanksgiving?"

"That would be fine," I said, "We'd enjoy having the youngster over. I'm so glad you called. We'll set two more places and be looking for you."

I hung up the phone, "John, I guess Mr. Wellington is coming after all. And he's bringing his grandson." I drifted downstairs not wasting time for further comment.

I was thinking now that he would be coming to dinner as soon as he could complete a couple of odd jobs. I was sure he'd make a hit with my family. He'd said the reason he hadn't called was because he hadn't known whether or not his grandson was coming from Texas. And he didn't want to tell me "yes" and then not show up. Well, I was certainly glad they both were coming.

I finally made it downstairs. Mother was all ready up and quietly peeling potatoes. She sat with her silvery curly strands drawn up off her face by a barrette at the back of her head. She looked strong sitting with her legs crossed at the ankle. Her full pink lips, dark brown eyes, and dark eyebrows looked exquisite without makeup. Oh course, her fingers, once long and attractive, had grown a few knots around several joints. But to go on, I told her she was a life saver. "What would I do without you?" I asked. "Still, you didn't need to peel these things. Kathy said she would do them."

Mother cleared her throat, "I guess I should have gotten the rest of these people up, but the time just got away from me. I figured there was more room to work here than in the kitchen." I had the happy thought of my family sleeping restfully, breathing in and out, all there in my home, all of us together in the silence as dawn burned the clouds away. It was a warm and cozy reflection and I wanted to further express myself on this matter. "You know, Mother, I enjoy having you at my house. Did you ever believe that you and Daddy, just two people in love, could become so many in number? As a child I always felt secure when you talked about Daddy and how much you loved him and how much he loved you. I really have missed him, you know."

Mother looked at me through misty eyes, "We have all really missed him. The truth is, I always wanted to build our dream home when your daddy was alive. You were just a young thing, six I believe." She cleared her throat. Mother didn't often cry, but she did at that moment. A feeling of love and empathy swept over me. I told her that I wasn't sad when Daddy died. It sounds cruel, but I didn't realize he'd be gone for so long. I really began to miss him when I was in high school when all my friends mostly spoke ill of their fathers. I asked Mother for the first time, "Why didn't you ever get married again to someone like Daddy?"

"Anne," she told me, "it was because I didn't think Steve or you girls would allow it. They were older than you and very protective. I remember a construction man wanting to call on me one day. He came to the house asking about me, but Jo wouldn't hear of it. She informed him, 'She's our mother! You leave her alone.' That was a long time ago."

Of course, with all the children married, I could see that circumstances could be different for mother now. Anyway, that day I asked her, "Do you ever get lonely? I mean, I know how hard it is for you to use your hands much anymore because of your arthritis. I know it's hard for you to cook. Maybe what you need is a man who can cook, clean, and build an elegant new house for you. You know, a man that measures up. After all Mother you're not too old."

Mother cleared her throat, "Good men are hard to come by. Besides, I couldn't live with a man; I don't need one and they cause too many problems!"

"Look at John, Mother," I told her, "he's a good husband. He provides a home for us and keeps us safe. What more should anyone ask for?"

You know how Mother always liked John. She would said, "Oh yes, I approve of John and love him as if he were one of my own. John is one of a kind; he does his duty." She said this day, "John is a lot like your daddy. That's why you married him, I imagine." Mother put down the peeled potato she'd been clenching in her hand.

To please Mother I said, "Yes, we are hanging in there, even after seven years of marriage. I don't know where I'd be without John." I didn't say anything more. John was very self-contained and so very quiet that there wasn't really very much to say about him. Almost nothing that would add to my mother's understanding of the way he was.

"I know that, Anne. I know that John is very quiet and reliable, but that's a good sort of husband to have. They don't talk much and maybe you might get lonely sometimes yourself, but believe me, it's good to have a reliable man to take care of the money end of things and to make sure that you and the children have what you need."

I thought about that for nearly a week afterwards. It seemed very sensible. But I wondered if all brides to be have that sort of sense. I would never have told my mother of any limitations that John had.

But there were times when John and I argued over such trivial things, such as visiting Mrs. Cunningham or my calling my friends on the phone. John had always thought that everything should be done just like his mother did them. And he was aware of his mother only in what he had observed of her. He thought that women weren't very complicated, I must say that. And when it came to my photography, well, that was something that John simply did not understand.

I know that John and I usually got along fine. But it was a question of never jarring his understanding. I wondered if my mother had felt that way about Daddy. What with her believing that John and Daddy were so much alike. Of course, I never remember my parents arguing, but I was too young to remember and I certainly didn't dare ask, and would never ask. It really wasn't my affair—despite the fact that I possessed that eternal curiosity, a curiosity, I'm sure many women have felt. What was the real truth behind a mother's high recommendation of the man her daughter had married?

But, the conversation did continue. I asked Mother, "What are you doing for Christmas? Do you have a man hidden away somewhere? After all, you're an attractive, vibrant woman. Maybe I'll have to find a man for you myself. I could be your matchmaker. Let's see, Uncle Jake is much too old for you, besides he already has a wife. Hmm. We have a nice one-armed widower who lives on the next block." Mother and I both thought of the movie, *The Fugitive*, when I said that. We had watched it on the VCR a day before and the two of us exploded into laughter. She didn't think she needed a man running from the law.

Kathy wandered on downstairs about that time. We were still giggling. "Don't you girls ever sleep? I need my beauty slumber."

Mother always defended all our looks. "Oh come now Kathy, you look beautiful whether you're sleeping, swimming, or hiking."

"That's right Kathy, look at me." I had to add, "I have to work hard at being attractive Miss Plain Jane in person."

"My hind foot," Kathy said. "You couldn't look ugly if you worked at it. You have lovely green eyes like our father. Your auburn hair is so shiny and looks great the way you're wearing it today, long and flowing. A sprinkling of exotic freckles and an exquisite classy nose like mine and Mother's, and perfectly shaped eyebrows which never need to be plucked." It was quite a buildup.

I wouldn't say I was homely, but I wouldn't say that I was more than just average. It's nice to hear one's mother and sister carry on, but to tell you the truth, I try to wear a little makeup so I don't appear too bland. I've always been happy enough with my external features. My mother's and sister's encouraging words naturally build confidence, but still I didn't have to be convinced absolutely that I was so gorgeous as all that. It was just wonderful to be able to luxuriate in the realization of the love that our family has one for the other.

At this point Mother spoke up again. "Well, I think all of our family members are quite good looking people." She cleared her throat, "And there's a reason for it. It's because we eat a variety of foods, including vegetables and good olive oil, not just sugar and bad fat." Mother was adamant. "Yes we are quite attractive folks except for Samantha," she added.

"Samantha who?" Kathy asked, stunned that her own mother would say anything derogatory of a family member.

Mother winked at me, "Don't you know who Samantha is? My dear, you're really missing out on life. She's JoEllen's new bulldog."

We all squealed with delight. "Well, I think all bulldogs are ugly, but we better not tell Jo about it," Kathy said. "Come to think of it, didn't we have a little watchdog beagle named Sam when we were kids, Mother?"

Mother scratched her head thinking a moment. "That's been years ago. Oh yes, I named him that because he had beautiful brown eyes like a cousin of mine named Sam." She cleared her throat again, "We called our dog Sam. I remember now," Mother said.

"Well, look I'm wide awake again," Kathy rolled her eyes around and then scrunched them up tight. She was doing her daily exercise routine.

Mother and I sat there entertained by the show. We knew this was part of Kathy's routine facial aerobics and it was quite comical how Kathy could twist her facial muscles into all sorts of weird shapes.

"I better jump in the shower before the water turns cold and then afterwards, I'll help with those dinner rolls and the grape salad," Kathy said.

"Would anyone like to go walking around the block with me?" I asked. All I got was blinks and smiles. "I better go upstairs then. Kathy, could you wake up your family and get them going. I really want to eat by 1:00." I ran part way up the stairs when it struck me that Mr. Wellington and his grandson were coming for dinner.

Pausing a moment, I went back down the steps to say, "Oh by the way Mama, Kathy, we have a couple of young men coming for Thanksgiving dinner and they could be here any time. You may want to put on your faces and get upstairs so you can entertain them while I'm preparing dinner." I quickly ran upstairs without explaining who the young men would be.

I overheard Mother say, "Did she say two young men? They must be the missionaries."

Little did she know we were having a young looking grandpa man and his grandson. I hoped at that moment that his grandson wasn't an obnoxious thirteen-year-old. I returned to the kitchen to wash my hands and prepare more food.

I had so much on my mind that day Sophie, and I even have very much on my mind today. There's always so much we could do and almost always so much to say. Always so much communication that could take place and yet, how much of what we think of in our deepest minds is ever experienced?

For example, take my photography. Speaking of photography, I got my camera out yesterday. I mean I took out all my equipment, the telephoto lens, everything! I even found my tripod. I thought that if I got them out, then I'd eventually get some film. I haven't had any film in my camera since I took some pictures of the boys at Christmas. I haven't even developed that roll yet. I simply threw it in the freezer so the film would stay fresh.

So, I realize that much of my life has been passed in the dream world. When I take the camera out, when I decide to use the camera, then very much of my dream world can become a real world. Is that what I want? I think so but I'm not sure.

Anyway, while I'm thinking of the dreams I have and the things I know how to do and could do, I must say, my buried treasure box of knowledge still stands pretty much silent and cold. Perhaps, people in general fear failure. They fear it simply because they don't want to try using their knowledge or following their dreams. They'd rather keep their treasures bound inside their souls and not bring them out for the world to see then sparkle. And am I any different from the rest of humanity? I don't know. After all, up to this point, I haven't really developed myself in line with the self that I think I am.

Some of these ideas in my head just go around and around like a carousel driven by immortal horses that never tire. So tell me again, Sophie, that I will do it one day. That perhaps now I'm ready to do it, to be the unique me. It's important that I know this at this point. You can't be aware of how important, but soon you will.

Well, I don't have time to think about it any longer now. I'll write more about the Thanksgiving Day events later.

Sorry I must retire my pen, but I must run. Time has slipped by and I have to pick up Shane from school. I almost forgot about my furnace. I guess we'll be eating supper at Mrs. Cunningham's this evening. The furnace man did call about an hour ago and said he would be right out. Ha! He better arrive soon so I can get over to my home after supper.

Love, Anne

P.S. Perhaps I truly have gone mad. But my dream. Doesn't that remind one of Halloween? Didn't you once read to me *The Eve of St. Agnes* by Keats. Was I dreaming as the young maiden in the poem? Let's reread the poem together. Is there a meaning there? A message for me?

TUESDAY FEBRUARY 27

Sophie,

At last, I'm back with pen in hand. To think it has been two weeks since I wrote last. There are reasons for this, and some accomplishments have been achieved during the interim. For one thing, the furnace finally is repaired and I'm feeling very content sitting in a warm house writing to you. We had a blizzard last night, so being warm's especially nice. It feels more than good to have a fire burning in the hearth again.

But, back to the passage of time. Though many days have gone by, I'm not sure I can account for all of them. At any rate, I'm sitting at my kitchen table as I write today. As I sit here, I have been studying the pearlized ceramic cherubs perched on the shelf beside the kitchen window. They make me think about the events of last Thanksgiving. Cherubs, yes. I met two cherubs that day. But I must tell you all about it. A grand day indeed, Thanksgiving Day! I wanted it to be a day never to forget and it was. The dinner and everything went very well. So to go back to that time, let me resume my story.

For the holiday weekend, I was so thrilled to see Kathy and her children again. Children indeed! They are mainly teenagers now. How did those little boys and girls grow up so quickly into tall men and women? Of course, I realize time doesn't wait for anyone, especially someone like myself who wants to re-experience the very good times such as last Thanksgiving Day.

I remember how Thanksgiving morning unfolded so marvelously. The turkey roasted in its juices all morning long. And I still recall the delicious aroma, sage and onion from the dressing mingled with the scent of fresh baked rolls. I made turkey gravy from the drippings. Food stood everywhere: Mother's shrimp cocktail; caramelized yams dotted with melting marshmallows, cranberries; Aunt Mamie's recipe for red grape salad; raspberries set in Jell-o.

The windows were steamed and had condensed sending little streams of water trickling down onto the window sill. My crystal chandelier trembled, casting away shadows from the dining room. The length of two tables united stood burgeoning into our tiled kitchen. Sparkling cranberry punch stood in glass pitchers ready to serve.

Food was sprawled upon the table in such quantities that dinner place settings were obscured by the items to be eaten. Chicago coleslaw, country potato salad, and carrot-raisin salad decked the adult end of the table. Stuffed green peppers sat on John's plate.

Mashed potatoes served in two bowls sat on opposite ends of the table, along with two bowls of my mother's famous turkey dressing, which had been baked around the sumptuous turkey. Two gravy boats sat by two platters piled high with meticulously cut white and dark turkey meat. One huge bowl of seven layer salad completed the dining offerings.

And, for decoration, there were two paper cup turkeys which Shane had made at school. The turkey platters stood perched on opposite ends of the table. In addition Ben had made some drawings of Indians and Pilgrims that I had secured with tape on the living room wall a week before Thanksgiving Day. Unfortunately, I had forgotten about the drawings in the bustle leading up to the Thanksgiving feast. Incidentally, have I all ready mentioned that Ben dreams of being an artist? He draws everything in the house; sometimes he draws on the walls of the house.

Back to the discussion of food—Sophie, you should have seen the pies; I had all kinds. The counter in the kitchen stood stacked with pies: pumpkin, cherry, apple, chocolate cream, and coconut cream. Well, am I making you hungry talking about all this food?

Regardless, as the food piled up, the valued guest piled in. JoEllen arrived with her family as we were placing all the food on the table. And it was so good to see each of them. They were an animated and loving pack, and once they had arrived, Sandy made her usual fuss over my boys. Sandy always has enjoyed watching my boys. And as you know since she has her driver's license, she can drive out to see us occasionally. JoEllen's family, what a wonderful bunch! Their arrival added to the hum of excitement and the sense of light and joy. And we were nearly ready to eat.

Soon thereafter, John stood at the end of the table in the living room and clinked the edge of his plate for attention. The meal was to begin. Everyone quieted down and a hush fell over the house. I was ready to stop bustling about in the kitchen. I took a big breath, sat down at the table, and closed my eyes for a prayer on the food.

But at that moment, the door bell rang. In the hubbub, I had forgotten about Mr. Wellington and his grandson.

Mother hadn't forgotten they were coming! "I'll let the young men in," she said clearing her throat. "John, don't bother, I'll get it." She stepped to the door.

Dear Sophie, you should have seen the look on Mother's face when she opened the door wide and was met by a grandpa-type man not much taller than herself and the other boy (Ha! Ha!) The boy was no boy. He was a man and a tall attractive one at that. He wore a black Stetson, a western-cut leather jacket and a snazzy pair of leather cowboy boots with gold insets. Mr. Wellington wore a brown suede jacket, looking quite different from his work clothes appearance. He wore Levi's with polished brown work boots.

Mother's face was a mixture of surprise and bewilderment. "Are you the two young men we were expecting?" she asked.

Mr. Wellington beamed back at the supposed compliment and said, "We are happy to accept the invitation for dinner." Then, noticing the bewildered look on Mother's face he asked, "Is this the John Olson residence?"

I had to look twice at this duo in the hallway and I wanted a closer look at the grandson. I hurried over to the doorway to rescue Mother as I greeted Mr. Wellington.

A closer look made my pulse quicken. The grandson was handsome as one of those mythical gods - like Adonis. His golden brown hair was neatly trimmed around his ears. His skin was flawless. His teeth were straight and white. He was the essence of manly vigor—my observations left no doubt that this grandson had to be near my age. But he was exceptional!! Over and above anyone I'd ever seen before.

He had a composed and gentle manner yet his facial features were rugged and tanned with days in the sun. He stood about six feet tall and was well proportioned. I stood momentarily captivated by his appearance. I had to force my attention to Mr. Wellington who was taking off his jacket to reveal a blue plaid shirt, which matched nicely with his sparkling blue eyes.

At that point, I turned to introduce my family to Mr. Wellington and then I stammered to the handsome grandson, "You must be . . . " All I could do was raise my eyebrows and smile. I felt stricken by the grandson's glorious appearance.

"Bradley Michael Wellington, Ma'am. It's a thoughtful gesture to allow us to attend this occasion." He nodded his head toward the crowd.

I nodded, too, and announced, "This is Bradley Michael Wellington. Bradley Michael, this is my family. It's a pleasure to have you join us."

"The pleasure's equal ma'am." He took a slight bow, lowered his black felt Stetson which he had clasped in one hand.

"Come right in," I said, "We are ready to sit down to dine." I tried not to stare, but to be as casual as would be normal. But once again I was halted by my gazing. The grandson's full mustache was neatly trimmed. I tried to refocus my attention, "Uh, uh, coats?"

Michael nodded, straightened up, took a deep breath and exhaled, filling out his fashionable western cut black and indigo shirt with an expansive fawn colored background. The shirt had tufts of leather tied in a knot over each breast. The details of style were unending. And he smelled of buckskin and *Oscar de la Renta*.

Mr. Wellington looked vivacious and healthy, his effervescent presence was appealing. He was not quite as old as I had imagined. Quite frankly, he seemed about my mother's age. Now, what was I thinking?

Well, whatever it was, I pushed it out of my mind to concentrate on what I should do next. I finally said to Walter, "Tell me, Mr. Wellington, have you purchased the materials for the dressers yet?" I tried not to stare at his grandson, but my curious feelings remained as I led the two men into the living room.

"Yes indeed, Anne, I have. Thank you for getting the measurement to me so quickly."

I knew how thrilled the boys would be to have a dresser of their own.

Mr. Wellington told me that Michael would be helping him with some large orders for Christmas and that there was plenty of time to finish the two dressers for Christmas.

I continued, "Mr. Wellington, Bradley Michael, we're just sitting down at the table."

The grandson politely extended his hand, "Call me Michael ma'am. My full name can be an obstacle for the message sender and the message receiver."

"And you can call me Anne," I said shaking his hand. I added, "because, that IS my name." I blushed.

Michael gave me a pleasant smile and another nod. I showed them where to wash up. As Michael turned sideways, I noticed a long scar that ran along his jaw line. An old scar. Had he been cut by glass? By a knife? At that moment I realized the man was mortal!

John spoke up above the buzz of voices in the room. "Okay family, let's gather around, the young ones can sit in the kitchen end. The adults will sit in the dining room end. Sandy, could you sit by Shane and Ben to help them?"

Sandy nodded. All gathered around the table. "Please be seated," John reiterated taking his seat at the head of the main table. I sat on the corner next to him to his right. Mother sat on the other side of John and Mr. Wellington was seated next to me, Michael sat next to my mother across the table from me.

Once we were all seated, John thanked the Lord for our bounteous blessing. Then he proceeded to begin the passing of the food around the table—a ten minute affair, at least. I watched the food traveling as if on a carousel. And I also watched what foods piled up on the two gentlemen's plates.

A few minutes later, when we were all eating, I looked around again. I caught Mother glancing over at Mr. Wellington and I saw him casually noticing her without letting on.

With that, my thoughts turned back to my first visit to see Mr. Wellington. On that day, in between discussing the dressers and our families in general, I had told him that my mother had been alone for several years. But I held no conscious thoughts that my mother and Mr. Wellington's two worlds would ever converge. And, yet, here they were, together now, glancing over at one another.

And myself? What was I doing? For one thing, feeling so flustered, I could barely eat. I had obviously been deeply affected by this man Michael. But I had no real idea why, so I determined to distract myself. I looked over at my husband, John. He was in high rare form and had nonchalantly reached over to Mother's plate to cut her turkey for her, "You shouldn't have to work so hard with that arthritic hand of yours," he told her. I had not even thought yet of doing the chore myself, a thing that I normally always spontaneously did.

John even struck up a conversation with the Wellington's. "Now where were you and your grandson raised? I hear that you're not originally from this area."

"As a matter of fact, I was born in corn country in Iowa." Mr. Wellington said, still smacking his lips in satisfaction from eating some of his food. "Yes indeed, I got married to a pretty young farm gal when I was 16 years old. That was about a hundred years ago. We enjoyed 14 years together. But Sally died suddenly at a very young age. She left me with four young ones to raise. Then when the children grew up and left home, I moved to Utah. First to Payson and then over to Springville. My daughter lives in Grantsville and so I've been trying to help her out this summer. I've been in Utah about twenty years now."

Mother was quietly listening to what Mr. Wellington was saying. Several of us watched as she smiled and nodded, giving her reaction to what Mr. Wellington was saying. Once or twice she cleared her throat and made short astute observations. "I know what you mean." And "Isn't this wonderful," etc.

A little further into the meal, I announced, "Now, would each of you please introduce the person to your left and tell us one thing you are thankful for." I started the round. "This is my husband, John Olson, who takes fine care of me and the boys. And I'm thankful for my mother who taught me how to think."

Mother gave me a grateful smile.

Then it was John's turn. He knitted his brow, introduced Mother as ". . . Abigail Ross, one of the finest cooks in the West. And added, "I'm thankful for my wife, Anne."

Next, Mother introduced Michael after asking for his full name. She was thankful, ". . . that we've had so much peace and contentment in the family this past year."

Michael introduced Kathy. Kathy presented her husband Bob and in a circle clockwise there were three of Kathy's boys Alex,

Lonny, and Gary who was one of the twins. Then there was Sandy at the end of the row; Ben on the end and starting back down the row, my Shane. Following these, there were three of Kathy's girls—starting with Sherri the twin to Gary. You remember my telling you of Kathy's twins don't you, Sophie? They are lovely children, all.

After Sherri, sat Tina and Cindy; oh, there were also Jo's two youngest girls and Kathy's two youngest children Jill and Sam. And on the other end of the table sat Nick and JoEllen; JoEllen introduced Mr. Wellington and said she was thankful for ". . . life, liberty, and the pursuit of going to the theater with Nick." We all chuckled.

Mr. Wellington was the last. He referred to me as "Miss Anne from Tooele, originally from Chicago." He was thankful that his grandson, Michael, could spend this fine day with him in a *real* family setting.

I know this may sound unbelievable, but with those words said, I'm sure I saw a tear slide down Michael's cheek. There had to be a story behind this and some depth of character, too. All response made, we sat and ate on and on until we were stuffed turkeys ourselves.

I should mention there were 22 people in all. The hum of voices nearly raised the roof, but we basked in the knowledge that friend and family could enjoy one day together of eating delectable food and giving thanks for our blessings.

Finally the meal was done. After savoring ideas and food for an hour or so, I hopped up to clear off the table. Sandy pitched right in to help. Michael got up, excused himself and started to clear the table too.

"No, you're our guest," I said adamantly. "You don't need to get up."

"Maybe so, ma'am, but really, I want to. I appreciate your kindness for inviting us to dinner today." Michael picked up a load of plates, passed close by me in the limited kitchen area. That moment, I felt something like electricity pass through my body. I shivered from the thrill of it. Michael set the dishes down on the counter, started filling the sink with hot water and suds. Then he stroked his mustache, rolled up his sleeves and said, "Ma'am, I want to do the dishes and listen to you do some telling about your life."

I couldn't refuse such an offer. Me tell about my life to a total stranger? Who had asked that of me before? Not a soul. I did feel flattered. I began talking. Finally I asked him if he was raised in Texas and, "What's the story of this fellow who is so much like his grandfather?" I asked.

"Well ma'am . . .," he stammered.

I touched him lightly on the forearm. "Please don't say 'ma'am', call me Anne."

He smiled, shuffled his feet a bit. Then he let his clear blue eyes meet mine. He looked into my eyes, his pleasant sounding voice started to sing like a familiar melody, "I was born in Texas and lived there till I was twelve. That's when my folks were killed in an airplane crash. It was quite a while ago."

I gave a little gasp at that news, bit at my lower lip. How could I express my comprehension of such a great tragedy? I didn't say a word; I continued to listen intently.

"My grandfather pulled me through," he said. "He moved to Texas to be my guardian. And he stayed with me until I graduated from Dallas High School. My grandfather also taught me how to cook, clean, and build out of wood nearly anything imaginable. Then, after going to college and receiving an education, I worked for a while as a computer programmer. But I soon tired of it and began working for a construction firm in California. With the knowledge of building that my grandfather had taught me, I enjoyed building things. And, anyway, I'd rather be working outside like Grandpa did than to be sitting inside an office all day. Well, that was nearly five years ago. I helped design and build several extraordinary homes near Lake Arrowhead in Southern California. Now I'm here."

"Well, you lead a pretty exciting life," I said.

He stroked his mustache again and said, "I don't much care for living in California. So, I returned to the Dallas area. There I own a modest ranch on the outskirts of Ft. Worth. I raise horses down there. I always dreamed of owning horses and a horse ranch and now that's become a reality," he said his eyes sparkling.

Hearing his story, I told him of my dreams, "I've always wanted to live on a ranch and have some horses of my own, too. My dad used to shoe horses on the side near Rockford. That was before he died. Back then, when I was young, my dad would take me with him to this large horse ranch."

Going back to when I was a child, you know Sophie, I'll never forget the smell of hay and horses at those stables. Oh, those days when Dad would take me with him. I remember Dad buying me a little cowboy outfit including red cowboy boots. This was for my fifth birthday. From that time on, I wanted to work with horses and be a cowboy. And Thanksgiving Day, talking to Michael, well, I talked on. I told him these previous old memories of mine while clearing off the table and cleaning up. We kept on talking to one another, nodding and listening in turn. At one point, when I came to a stop he said, "You lost your father when you were six?" Then he seemed to be studying my face. After that, he added, "I bet that was pretty tough?"

"I don't dwell on it much," I replied. "Mother misses Daddy and she gets extremely lonely at times—but she never mentions it. In general, she cusses all men and she has never remarried." I began scraping leftovers from a big pile of plates. I scraped them into a big bowl.

Michael brought more plates to the sink nodding thoughtfully all the while. Finally he said, "Well, Anne, why don't you raise horses here in Tooele? There's lots of horses around this area, and land too. Utah raises some of the finest horses in the nation."

I was dumbstruck, Sophie. I'd never thought of it as a possibility and I told him that. I also said, "I guess you kind of get stuck in one mode in life and forget there's anything else beyond it."

"Well, Anne, actually, I don't break horses. I have a couple of wranglers who train them for me. But, I have a good riding horse."

"What's his name?"

"Oh, you mean my horse's name?" Michael's mustache turned up into a smile, "Her name is Annie."

"What? You have a horse with MY name?"

He laughed and said, "Oh, I named her after Annie Oakley." He stroked his mustache while plates clattered around us. "But back to the subject. The two wranglers who train my horses do a good job. I primarily breed thoroughbreds and then I sell them. Once in a while I build a house or two when I get itchy hands for two by fours and a nail gun."

There was a long pause about then. I felt so drawn to this stranger that I sank into a period of silence. He had such a powerful force of energy like that of a giant magnet. And he seemed familiar, like someone I'd known before. I looked into his eyes. With that, our eyes locked briefly. My heart gave a little jump and I quickly looked away and down to the floor.

Michael said, "Well, Anne, I guess I'd better round up some more dishes. But I want you to know that this day has meant a lot to me. Just being accepted into a family circle and having a feeling of belonging. I never had that you know. I never had any brothers or sisters, just Grandpa. I also have a few cousins, but we never lived close enough to stay in contact." With that, he stepped to the table for more dishes.

Misty the cat was suddenly standing outside the window, meowing for leftovers. I scraped some juicy tidbits from the plates onto another plate and took some food out to her. I was happier than usual doing this; so full was I of the vibrant spirit of this man inside my house. He had been a delight, a big help with the dishes, an encouragement for life overall. I felt full of fire and ice, fed my cat with a sense of bountifulness and joy.

This was not a totally unknown experience for me, Sophie, I had felt something like this before. It was the feeling that comes when you truly love another person for that person's passion, ideas, personality, character. It was the feeling I had back years ago when I met John and realized that he, such a steady, reliable man, was to be by husband. But why was this feeling re-emerging inside my heart now? I was a married woman—a happily married woman. It was confusing to me.

Standing there in the kitchen that very moment, I tried sorting things out in my head. Maybe the feeling was new in nature. Maybe it was simply a reaction to discovering a real person who cared about values, a person who was generous and giving. Perhaps I was in contact with a kindred spirit. The man certainly fit in perfectly, like family. But I couldn't continue to grapple with the matter. I wanted to get the dishes of food off the table and the board games on: Scrabble, Monopoly, and Life—all games the family could enjoy.

When I walked into the living room to see if everything had been cleared off, there in the front room on the love seat sat Mother and Mr. Wellington. I had to blink a couple of times. I couldn't believe it. But I saw the two of them sitting right there – together side by side. They were carrying on like two old friends, laughing and smiling, discussing with one another the events of their lives. Instantly, it occurred to me that the two were close to the same age, had two life times to share, one with the other. Of course, I didn't want to interrupt; I kept my thought to myself. I went on about my business which was gathering up more dishes and hauling them to the kitchen sink. Back again in the kitchen, I once more came in close proximity to Michael. My face turned crimson. I struggled for something to say. "I enjoyed reading your grandpa's poetry." I stammered. "I write a little poetry myself as a hobby, but doesn't everyone?" I tried to sound casual. I hoped he hadn't noticed my repeated fits of blushing.

With a twinkle in his eye, Michael said, "Anne, I'd like to write a hot romance novel where the love was burning like a strip of lightning from beginning to end."

"Well..." I said, nearly dropping the plates I held. Where was my husband when I needed him? At that moment, I heard a banjo tune strike up downstairs and a harmonica; I realized John wouldn't be upstairs to intervene. I busied myself with the dishes.

I decided to save dessert until later. The cousins had mainly gone outside to play horseshoes and Frisbee Tag. Outdoors there was plenty of room for them to roust about while the sun was streaming through the typically cerulean sky.

Sandy had brought the last of the plates and platters from the table, her sister, Patty, attending to the cleanup details. Now the two of them were sponging the table clean and sweeping up the floors.

Thinking of cleaning up and aprons, I went to the kitchen linen drawer and pulled out some aprons to give to the girls, "So your clothes don't get soiled," I said to both of them. With that, Michael asked if there was an apron for him. I pulled out two more aprons and held them up. "Would you prefer the floral pink or the lavender one?"

"Do you have an old dish towel? I'll tie it around in back."

I went to the drawer and grabbed up an old flour-sack dish towel.

He quickly slipped the towel from my grasp. Then he wrapped it around the front of him and tied it in back very securely with a square knot.

Right then, I asked Michael if he'd ever been married.

"No, not exactly," he said.

Well, as you can imagine Sophie, I raised my eyebrows questioning his meaning. It wasn't an interrogation. I'm sure he realized he didn't have to answer anything he didn't want to. But what he had to say was very interesting. Listen to this.

"Once I thought I was in love with a girl," he said. "It was when I was nineteen. She was supposed to be a pretty good friend of mine. One day she told me that she was going to have a child fathered by a drug addict. Well, I thought I'd be gallant by taking care of her since the other man certainly didn't want anything to do with her. So we quickly set a date and got married. But, I soon found out she had lied to me—she was never actually pregnant. She had done it on a bet of some sort. And, thus I had the marriage annulled a week later."

Of course, Sophie, in my mind, this made Michael just as vulnerable as the next fellow to degenerate women. I said to him, "Unlucky in love huh?"

"Lucky in not loving any women," he said. "Anne, I hate to admit it, but my heart became a stone after that. And I haven't had time to put down roots and find a lady who'd like to spend a lifetime with a man like me."

And you know, Sophie, what a sucker for romance I am in my heart, but I tell you, I can't believe what came out of my mouth next. "Really?" I asked. "Well just for the record, if I was single and looking, I'd certainly want to find out more about what makes you tick. Boys like you are hard pressed for competitors in your league. You're just way out there on your own. It's so good to meet someone who is so normal and wholesome."

His mustached lips turned up into a thoughtful smile. His clear eyes swept over my face again. He really was intent on studying my face. It didn't make me feel uncomfortable though. He told me that he didn't get out much, but that he enjoyed visiting his Grandpa Walter. He said, "Grandpa has been a huge influence for good in my life. Where have all the good old gentlemen gone these days? Do they still exist?"

"Trust me," I told him, "they still exist. We have a lot of older gentleman that have been a fine example in my life. For instance, John's family is packed full of good men. Maybe they just don't have any left in the big city."

"Back to the subject of women," Michael said. "Most girls, Anne, want only looks, glamour, money, and the fast life. It can wear a man down. I'm happy with raising horses. Horses demand little and they do me a world of good simply working with them. Alas, horses sure can tell when you're good to them and treat them with respect and kindness. I strictly treat my horses like the high-bred animals they are. And they don't talk back."

At that point Sophie, I felt glad that Michael had come over with his grandpa, and I told him so. I said, "At least, for Mother's sake, I'm glad you both came." I told him to take a look in the front room. I led him by the arm to the doorway to the living room, pointed to the duo with my chin, then casually as I finished gathering a couple of serving bowls and took them to the kitchen.

When Michael came back to the kitchen his eyes were snapping with energy. "What do you make of that, Anne?" He sounded incredulous.

"What do you make of it?" I asked then I whispered, "You see, Mother claims she hates men." We both chuckled softly like two children with a secret.

At that instant Shane burst into the kitchen. He was scratching his ear lobe, "Hi Mama, when do we get to eat pie?"

"Well, we can have it any time you want." I said. "Are you going to play outside or inside after eating pie?"

"Oh probably inside," he said tugging at his ear lobe. He turned his attention to Michael. "I really like your shirt." He jumped up to turn on the water tap for a drink, filled a cup, and jumped down. Then eying Michael he continued, "...but I think your mustache looks kind of..."

I looked at Shane hoping he wouldn't make a rude comment.

". . . silly." Shane rolled his eyes for emphasis, drank his water.

"Shane, I'll call you when the pie is ready," I said emphatically.

Michael bent down to Shane's height, raised his eyebrows and said, "Well, sir, do you think my mustache is a little too much?" He closed one eye, hoping for a response about his mustache.

"Well, maybe not," Shane said. "You might look worse without it." Then he strode out of the room tugging at his ear. So, much for the expert opinion of a six-year-old.

I, of course, told Michael not to take any of Shane's comments personally. And I told him I thought his mustache made him look engaging and wise.

"Kind of like an old mountain guru?" he said.

"Oh yes," I said, "the sage of the century!"

We had a good laugh. I asked if he was best at cutting or serving pie?

"I do both with equal flourish," he replied. But then he opted to cut the pie. And I served it up. Soon most everyone had bustled back into the dining room like starved penguins to their feed. It was one of the routine ways of eating for us, thus assuring us on Thanksgiving Day that we had plenty to eat and it was all delicious.

Mother and Walter floated into the dining room with dreams like moonbeams emanating from their eyes. And Michael dug into his piece of pie. I was speechless, but I was quite, quite happy about this turn of events.

After they had eaten more pie at about 6:00 p.m., Walter and Michael reluctantly thanked us all for the delightful day and said goodbye. They sauntered out the front door and climbed into Walter's green pickup. They waved to us. Mother and I waved back to them from the porch.

John had come and gone with the ebbing food eaters and had now returned to give banjo lessons to whoever was interested back downstairs. There was still a festive feel to the air.

I took Mother by the hand and squeezed it tight, "Well, my dear," I told her, "it looks like you had a good time."

"I always have a good time with my family," she answered after clearing her throat.

She would not admit anything about Walter. Okay, she could play the uninterested maiden. Ha! At that moment, I felt like something big was going to happen at Christmas time. I wondered if Cupid was shooting little arrows inside my house.

So, Sophie, this past Thanksgiving was a wonderful day as you can see. But then, that next Monday after Thanksgiving, I realized that I was going to have a baby. John and I both agreed to tell no one until I was at least three months along. I was hoping for a girl and also excited about the prospects of having a new addition to the family.

All was quiet until the next thing happened and the next and so on. Right here, I can tell you that Mother had been invited for lunch over at Walter's place twice that week following Thanksgiving Day. And Michael had driven over to pick her up both times.

During these pickup visits, I learned that Michael was well versed in many areas of learning. And Mother learned more of it as she rode along with him. Also, the boys were entranced with him. I wasn't sure what Mother and Walter were cooking up, but as a family, we were beginning a wonderful friendship with both of these men. One of the reasons that Mother had wanted to go to Walter's she said, was to go with him to help purchase odds and ends for finishing the boys' dressers for Christmas. Going with Walter to get building material became a key focus for her for a couple of days.

Oh, and I received a little thank you note in the mail from Michael that next week. The card had a picture of a horse with a farm house in the background. Michael wrote on the card, *Thank you for making me a part of your family. It was a Thanksgiving Day I'll never forget.* Signed *Michael.* The words brought a warm feeling to my soul. I remembered how he had helped me with the dishes. Of course, Thanksgiving was an important day, but then it faded from my consciousness.

With Shane back in school that next Monday, Mother read books to Ben, all of which helped me get Christmas items ready.

Then the time came for us to put up our Christmas tree. It had been customary to put up the tree and trim it the week following Thanksgiving on that weekend. John ran our house a great deal like his parents had run theirs. For example, John and I had agreed that a few gifts throughout the year were better than hundreds of gifts at Christmas which would go unappreciated. Usually we planned on one or two large gifts for each person. This year was no exception to our ideas.

I'd asked Walter during the week if he had a pattern for wooden rocking horses which I could paint after they were cut out to use as tree ornaments. He said he didn't but that Michael could design something and make the cutouts for me. Well, Walter was right. Michael came over and drew up a design for me. Then he cut a few dozen rocking horses out for me to paint. At the same time he told me more about his life. I listened intently to what he said, kept my distance though, well on the up and up and trying not to revive Thanksgiving Day fire and ice, in other words—passion and chills running up my spine. He evidently did the same. We were able to talk and interact as respectable adults.

That following Thursday and Friday, I kept busy painting rocking horse ornaments. The boys were thrilled with them. I let Ben and Shane each paint one and I put their names on the pair that they had made. The work turned out darling. John even had commented on the darling painted horses. I had them all ready to hang on our tree by Saturday.

On the night before our big decorating spree, John had taken the boys over to get a real pine tree at one of the local places. It was after dark by the time they had gotten the tree home. The full tree that John had selected scented the house with elegant pine aroma. I was enjoying the delightful aroma, looking at every angle of the tree when Shane informed me, "Dad scraped the side of the pickup on a fence post leaving the parking lot." I raised my eyebrows in amazement. I wasn't prepared for John to do such a thing as this. He was always such a competent driver. But in all the excitement, I didn't bring the matter up for discussion with John.

When Saturday morning arrived, the boys, John and I were up early to decorate the Christmas tree. John and I went in to the living room to see where we would put the tree. The boys ran to the hall closet to retrieve garlands and lights, their spirits flying high with excitement.

John began setting the tree in the stand, when suddenly he stumbled and caught himself from falling. I hadn't known him ever to be clumsy or careless. I was astonished. I helped him lower the tree to the floor but I wanted the boys to help their dad with the tree. "Boys, would you like to help put the tree up," I called. About this time, Walter drove into the yard in his green pickup truck.

At the door, Walter asked if "Mama" was home. I had to kid him a little, "I am home, what do you want?"

He smiled and rubbed his chin, "Not you Mama! Your Mama—Abigail."

I could see he was holding something behind him and I was anxious to find out what it was. "What tidings do you bring this day for my mother?"

He smiled shyly, "You'll have to wait to find out." He stood there beaming like a school boy with a polished apple for teacher.

"Are you planning on staying to help decorate the Christmas tree?"

"Yes, of course," he told me. But then he went on to say, "I believe Abigail invited me to this momentous occasion. I wondered if John could use a hand with putting up the tree. I hear it's a good-sized tree."

Walter stepped into the house, adjusting his spectacles as he walked. "Now, do I get to see Abigail or not?" He chuckled nervously as he stood in the hallway.

I went immediately then to the living room to talk to John, but he had disappeared. I thought perhaps he'd gone to get some tools. The tree lay still sprawled in the living room in the same place.

I called out, "Mr. Wellington, Walter, I like you. Thank you for bringing out the best in my mother. I'm so glad we met that one day in the store. The day you sang your song."

"Yes, indeed," he said, stepping my way, "that was a fine rainy day, a marvelous day! But I never thought I'd see you again." Walter gave a half smile, closed his eyes a moment. Perhaps he was thinking of something of import. I told him I'd get Mother. His eyes opened wide with anticipation.

"Walter, I hope you keep coming by. I'll go see if she's ready."

I scurried downstairs, found Mother in the family room flipping through a Christmas catalog. As I greeted her I told her she looked terrific in her new sweater. "By the way," I said, "you have a charming visitor upstairs. He's anxiously awaiting your presence."

"Oh my, is Walter here?" she said clearing her throat.

To me, Mother was acting strangely. "Mother, don't feign ignorance," I told her. "He's here so don't keep him waiting. Of course he's here!" I tried to get a grip on things. "We need a heart to heart talk about your situation," I commented.

She cleared her throat again, "Oh Anne," she said, "he's so . . . " she waved her hands as if trying to find the words to describe her feelings. Finally, she said, ". . . fun. Did you know we're the very same age. He's a couple of months older than me. We graduated from high school the same year. We have a lot in common."

"So! Well, what are you afraid of?" I asked. Sensing that Mother might be worried about my opinion of Walter, I added, "Mother, it really doesn't matter how I feel. It's important how he makes you feel and how you make him feel. But I heartily approve. I had no idea you two matched up so completely. And he is charming, handy, he cooks, the works. He could build you a house wherever you'd like to live. Have you discovered anything that you don't like about him?"

"Oh, my darling Anne, what are these feelings?"

"It's called love, Mother. It's been a little while, but you remember. You two little lanterns have lit up the world around you."

Mother cleared her throat once again, "You know how I've always said that I'd never have another man in my house for as long as I lived . . ."

"I must have amnesia," I cut in. "Have I heard these words before? I don't remember them! Mother, just get upstairs and love that wonderful man up there. He's your oasis. You've been stranded. You need this living spring. Go!"

"Do I look all right?" She gave a little sniff.

"Mother you look terrific! By the way, is that new perfume?"

"L'fleur." She fluttered her eyelashes, paused momentarily with her one hand on hip, one hand over her head.

"Go get him Tiger!" I let her go ahead. I didn't want to rush upstairs and ruin the moment. I soon heard excited voices as if two old friends had been reunited for the first time in years. I wondered what course Mother was planning to take. I'd never seen her in love with anyone except Dad. And that was far in the past. I wondered if anything would come of this sparkling new alliance. In my heart, I hoped something good would come of it. I felt like the child who'd become the nurturer of her own mother at that moment. And I loved Mother for her candid way of dealing with the problem.

So, that day turned out to be a very busy day and passed rapidly. Then, that evening after all the decorating, I looked around to find that the house sparkled and twinkled with little clear Christmas lights glistening in the window, on the tree, around the banister. The tree was decorated in red and white. Throughout, it was hung with the hand-painted rocking horses and little silver bells all in stunning array. With Mother and Walter pitching in, the grand décor was done. I was worn out completely but feeling very joyous inside, indeed.

After the boys were in bed, John and I sat on the sofa admiring the exquisite decor. There really was a feeling of love and goodwill stirring within the room. We could rest in peace. John was quietly holding my hand as we gazed upon the bright picture in serenity, while recounting our blessings at this time of the year. All was calm and brighter than I could hope for.

"What a day, Anne," John said, knitting his brows. "Now it seems very interesting to me that your mother and Walter seem to be very good friends. But, I can understand. I like Walter myself. He's a very solid person and of course, so is your mother. I'd like to spend some time talking with Walter. He's very handy and knows how to do many things."

"Yes," I relied, "Walter is handy and Mother is an interesting person. I didn't say anything about their budding romance. Obviously John didn't look at it in those terms, although he noticed some bond developing between these two people.

"I hope nothing spoils the fun of either one of them, or for us or anyone," I told him. "It's wonderful to see them so animated and so full of happiness and anticipation. Also, John, did you notice that Walter brought a dozen red roses for Mother? Red roses. Now that's a very nice thought," I added.

"Well, yes—but it's pretty extravagant. I don't know about people who buy red roses. It seems a bit frivolous."

"Oh, well," I replied, "it's not necessary. Not for a practical girl like me."

He knitted his brows again, "That's right, and don't you forget that this is the way we want to be."

We sat in front of the fireplace with the logs burning down. "Oh I won't forget that we must be practical," I told him. "In fact, you remember when we first moved here? You bought twelve Simplicity roses for a rose hedge. They bloom just fine and bloom and last all summer long. They bloom and bloom the entire season while the weather is good, year every year."

"That's right," he said," and now they have made a nice wall on the south side of the yard."

"Having that wall prevents people from walking into the yard," I added. John was pleased that he'd built a wall. Walls kept things in their own secure world.

We sat for nearly an hour in quiet reflection. Yes, I did feel safe in John's world even though I knew it was small. I thought at that moment, this is my secure life. I stared into the fireplace, watched the logs turn to ashes, realized it was time to retire for the evening. But, at that moment, in my mind, I stored a photograph of John sitting next to me on the sofa, surrounded by Christmas ornamentation. John, solemn and quiet, bothered by his headache perhaps. Not wanting to do or say too much but trying to respond to the event. I guess Sophie, that's how I will always remember John. It was a sort of perfect evening with him. The night was dark and cold. Yet, with no cloud cover, the stars twinkled brightly in the crisp air. I closed the curtains that evening, and I felt at peace inside, unaware as to what the next day might bring.

Monday morning before John drove off to work, the two of us at the breakfast table, John wanted to sit for a moment to reminisce about the old days, to recall the time of our courtship, that day at college when we first met, to relive even the day he had proposed marriage to me?

What a day of high adventure that had been Sophie—you and I had gone to the airstrip when John and his friend took me up in a plane and there he asked me the great question, as you recall. A roommate of John's was learning to fly and invited us to fly with him after he'd gotten his license. So the day had come but there was a surprise with it.

John had several friends and classmates on the ground near the airstrip. The crowd had made a formation, which spelled out "Anne marry me! J. Olson." He pointed out the message. I was thrilled, screamed "Yes, yes" in his ear.

It was an exciting time, a big show. But what I saw in it was not so much John's own imagination, as the effort of all his friends to help him propose. It was a sweet time of talking. I felt at peace inside, confident that my life was right on track. I loved John. I did. Quiet, solemn man that he was. And I loved my two boys. And as we sat sipping hot cocoa that morning, I remember John saying, "Anne I am glad I married you." It was just one of those moments of taking a picture in my head of how things were – a slice in time of my life with John. I had no inkling that events could shift so abruptly and that my secure world could crumble around me.

John left at 8:00 o'clock for work as usual. What followed is a difficult story to tell. Please sit down as you read this. I don't remember if I mentioned this earlier to you, but, John had complained a couple of months prior to this time of having headaches. But on the day I am describing to you, John was driving home from work. He had taken the route along the lake on the Reno road. There he clipped a post. His car sailed off the overpass onto the freeway below. Quickly the police had blocked off the interstate road, then, ambulances and rescue trucks clogged the main artery. And John? He flew to heaven. The impact had killed him instantly, they reported to me later.

I realize that this is the first time I'm telling you of John's death, but I must tell it to you my way. Let me go on to say now that the autopsy showed that John had a brain tumor which doctors agreed had probably been the source of his headaches. More importantly, it had affected his sense of balance. He probably never even knew what happened to him.

I cried inconsolably after Officer Miller stopped by the house that evening to inform me about John's accident. I said something like, "Are you sure?" I didn't believe him at first. I could not believe that John could die. He was too young. He was MY husband. He had two children and a wife to care for. He had a new baby to care for come summer!

I'm just grateful that Mother was staying at the house with me at the time. She cried as much as I did. The boys cried, but I think they were more scared than anything. I don't think they realized what was happening. They knew that their father wasn't home. I tried to explain it. But I don't think they really understood. I told them that their daddy was home with Heavenly Father.

Over the next weeks John's employer and co-workers sent cards saying they were sorry. Mrs. Cunningham wept, the whole Olson family cried out in anguish, and, indeed all of Tooele mourned the passing of John Olson. He was laid to rest in the city cemetery, in the lot with four generations of Olson family members. The relative's place was on the east side of town under the knoll.

Now, as to Walter and Michael, if it hadn't been for their strength and understanding, I don't know what we would have done. With Christmas just around the bend, I didn't know what we were going to do. I felt weak, walked around the house in a daze. But I made it through the funeral holding on to my two boys and thinking of John's baby inside me. I cried for a week, two weeks. I don't exactly remember. My world had turned upside-down and fell upon me crushing out the breath of life as I had known it.

It wasn't fair. How could it happen to me? I kept asking. Each night I cried out, to my mirror in the bedroom, "John can't die!" Then I'd think of my brother Steve and John and how they were as a great duet to my ears. And since Steven was gone, how John's melody was necessary to carry me! Now I believed the sublime strain of music would rise no more.

Tears flowed down my face, and numbness swept through my body like a chilling frost. Then there was silence. Silence so loud, that the tumult reverberated in my eardrums. The earthquake of my soul roared. I wondered if I could bear this ordeal. *Who would I lean on? What would I do?* I was alone and frightened.

What was the larger picture? What was that phrase I'd often heard in college about *carpe diem*? My brain seemed sucked into a black hole. The thought occurred to me how often philosophical men sermonize that, "All men are born and all men will die." Of course it was true. And I had realized that all men would die. But not John! How could John have died? I felt like a person who finds herself the sole survivor of a plane crash.

All I knew was that I had to cope with one minute at a time, one hour at a time, one day at a time. And I'd nearly forgotten about Christmas. Everyone would be celebrating Christmas! Except me. They'd have their parties and fun. And then there I was. I don't know if you can understand how I felt. It was a pathetic state I found myself in. I locked myself in a little cage with sorrow and fear as padlocks to hold me. And, tearfully, I wondered what each waking moment would bring.

My dear, I hate to quit here. I am too drained to write more. My pulse throbs and my nerves are gone haywire. I must do more quiet thinking and praying. Please know I do care about you. And thank you so much for caring for me. I do appreciate you. I'm sorry that this is the first time hearing of this news, but I was simply a lost child in a dream world after John's passing. I lost all my senses and connections to the real world.

As always, Anne

FEBRUARY 27 LATER

Sophie, here I am writing to you again. It is night time of the same day. I have so many thoughts to share with you. And when I take a break from the writing in order to devote myself to daily chores, my mind teems with ideas and issues that I have yet to share with you. Now the house is quiet. I'm sitting here in my bedroom at my desk sipping some steaming hot lemon blossom tea. I feel soothed and the boys are in bed asleep. I am able to write again.

I want to tell you my story in the right order and with the right emphasis and with all the points that I reflect upon. It's hard to do, but an atmosphere like this does enhance the effort. I want you to know how I am bearing the burden of what has happened to me and yet how I'm filled with aspirations and a sense of the forthcoming fulfillment of my dreams.

First, I want to go back to the past, to the time when John got in the terrible accident. Truly Sophie, I was despondent when that event occurred. I was not prepared for it. I couldn't comprehend the fact that John wasn't coming home for supper again. I'd grown accustomed to *same old, same old*. I could not understand that our relationship on this earth had ended. John was a very solemn and quiet man and I suppose in many ways he had his short comings. But from the day that I married him, to the present time that I lost him, it never occurred to me that there would be any other person in my life. I was satisfied with my convictions in this matter.

Of course, at the time that the fatal accident occurred, the weather gave me little opportunity for reprieve. The day following the funeral, we had a huge blizzard. Snow and cold shut out the light of day. Icicles hung from the eaves of the house facing the road. Snow weighed down the pines, maples, and Chinese elms that grow along the street. Sidewalks and roads became clogged with snow. Cars, vans, trucks which lined the street and filled the driveways, seemed great blurs of white with a greater blur of white.

That day after the funeral, the wind howled, and leaves too stubborn to fall with autumn gusts were torn away from the branches. Flung to the ground, they lay buried under layers of snowflakes clustered together as one great ocean of white. Wind howled from the east down the canyons and across the valley with frantic blast. With the raging wind, I huddled on the sofa with hands clasped tight trying to be brave. I fought against the idea that all hope and vision had been lost in a wasteland of white, blinding chilling white.

I appreciated the fact that neighbors brought all kinds of food to fill us physically. In fact, there was an unbelievable parade of foodstuff arriving: potato salads, homemade chicken noodle soup, pot roast dinners, cakes, and cookies by the tray load. I don't remember even turning on the oven during the entire ordeal. But I really had no taste for anything. I ate only because my baby needed nourishment and I because needed to have energy for my boys.

I thought of John—of his banjo lying silent gathering dust. And I truly missed his music; I longed for his music to soothe my heart. I had tried to imagine that he was on an extended journey to some foreign land. It made it easier at first. I had written letters to him, sealed them, and then burned them in the hearth. It helped to ease the pain that stuck in my heart like a knife.

And as I think about it now, I was so distressed that I shut out my children, friends, Mother, Walter, everyone. I did this as one might pull down a Venetian blind to shut out the light. I didn't realize it, but now I see that this is what I did. I believed I wanted to die with John! I questioned why he hadn't taken me with him. I believed perhaps, I could not face the future alone. What was I, a wife and mother, to do without a husband? Alone, I inwardly was howling, desperate and howling against my circumstances. I considered myself desperate, bound down with tight cords of insecurity and hopelessness, feeling overwhelmed and unable to achieve anything of significance without the security of John as an anchor in our lives and our stable family household.

I think it was a normal state for a widow, I see that now. I couldn't see it then. I held close to my box of tissues in one hand and a two-quart container of milk in the other. I was reveling in sorrow and pity. Misery became my motto. It's a good thing something extraordinary finally happened. And that it came in the form of a vision.

About a week before Christmas I had a dream. I remember feeling numb as though my senses were dead. During that night I tossed and thrashed around in bed for hours. I felt an overwhelming sadness envelope me, tears soaked my pillow. Sleep finally carried me away in my darkest hour, when suddenly this vision leapt from obscure darkness into bright awareness and roused me.

John appeared to me. He stepped toward me and gathered me in his arms. I was thrilled to see him. I stopped crying but broke from his arms and stared at him. I searched his eyes. Although I was thrilled to see him, he seemed downcast and laden with sorrow. He took my hand and looked at me gently. He said, "Anne, don't cry for me anymore. I'm all right. Get on with living and be happy. Life is a gift. Give of yourself."

His facial features were not as harsh as I remember them to be in life, yet, it was clear that he was distressed. And I guess that was it, the message I mean. What he said affected me deeply. All of a sudden, in this dream, I found myself inside a gift wrapped box with a big ribbon on top. I could see myself inside the box. He added, "Remember the living. Please take care of Shane and Ben. But please, no more tears! I cannot take your weeping for me any longer." He kissed my hand and he was gone.

I awoke from this dream with a start. And right then, with renewed will, I told myself to stop crying. I was all cried out by this point anyway, and I resolved at that moment to get hold of myself. I must say, Sophie, this dream helped me get through the holidays. I threw out my box of tissues. I tried to get a grip on life once again. I didn't know how I would ever be the same again. But with realizing that John was all right, a new feeling of peace swept over me. I now felt that I would survive somehow. I believed that I could go on with life as John had instructed me to do. He wanted happiness for me and he wanted no sorrow for either of us.

The morning following this dream, Walter and Michael drove up. Loaded in the back of Walter's pickup were the two new dressers for the boys. The dressers looked magnificent from the window, maple finish just as I had asked. I pushed my sadness completely from my mind. I was thrilled to realize that a project so recently begun, so recently no more than an idea in my mind, had now become a reality. Seeing this final product was something akin to viewing the ocean for the first time. It was a miraculous awakening that washed over me. And it offered a sure broadening of my point of view.

Walter and Michael came to the door. I smiled as I greeted them, trying to show them that I was appreciative and happy. No longer did I want to cry and weep and moan as I had done for days. I invited them both in for some hot cocoa and they readily accepted. I watched Michael's every movement. He moved with fluidity and poise. Once inside the door, he asked, "Anne, may I hang up my coat in your closet?" He was one step ahead of me.

"Certainly," I replied. With that, Michael took Walter's coat as well as his own and hung them in the hall closet. I don't know why this struck me as such a significant thing. After all, that is what a hall closet is for. But it did strike me nonetheless. A renewed sense of security was beginning to sweep over me.

When Mother heard the hall door close she came upstairs. She hurried toward Walter just as a teenager might rush toward her beau on Prom night. She was animated and full of news to tell Walter. Again, I felt the realities of my loneliness. With John gone, I could not hope to have someone that I could rush to, into whose arms I could rush. My heart suddenly felt heavy. Would it be this way the rest of my life?

A young widow is a widow no less. And one has to consider the question, *will I ever marry again? Will I ever have a husband again? A companion?* John said for me to be happy, but what was I supposed to do? So many thoughts were tugging at my heart. I wasn't sure what my true position was regarding love. I wasn't sure what my true feelings were.

But then, I thought of Michael's coat hanging next to mine in the closet. I liked the idea of his coat touching mine. I caught myself thinking of this. Then I got a grip on things. I thought *what a joyous time right now to be alive, a new day had dawned.* I silently thanked God for sending these gentlemen to my house to lighten my mood and perhaps help me to realize John's instructions for me.

Quick enough, we all moved into the kitchen, drank our cocoa. And before I even knew it, the men pulled on their coats and off they went to haul the dressers into the garage. They secured the furniture in the garage and covered the pieces with a tarpaulin. I was thrilled that the dressers had arrived, but I truly longed to see them completely in place inside the house.

As I told you, during that week we had had several overcast days. But with the last blizzard the snow had hit with such fierce velocity snow was whipped up into tall drifts over the fence posts. This particular morning, with the winds at a standstill, the clouds soon dissipated, the sun emerged and a whole new glistening world opened up outside.

With the sun suddenly breaking the darkness barrier, dazzling icicles sparkled like crystal prisms. The trees stood like frozen guards with ice and snow clinging precariously on one side. The sunlight striking the tree limbs soon turned the ice into rivulets of water. At least eight inches of snow lay on the ground with new snow drifts tucked up around bushes and street curbs.

After the men had the dressers in place, Michael offered to help with snow removal while Walter sat on the sofa a moment waiting for Mother to come back upstairs. I thought that it would be helpful to have the snow removed from the walks and so I told Michael I appreciated his offer to help. That was a job that John would have done. And now, here was Michael doing the job for me, taking over John's job.

Ben asked if he could go outside with Michael to shovel the sidewalk. I told him that would be fine if it was all right with Michael. I was convinced that Ben wanted merely to climb the drifts and roll in the snow. Of course Michael agreed to have Ben as a companion. I told Michael where to find the snow shovel and he headed outside. But I gave Ben additional instructions before I'd let him leave, "Ben, you need to bundle up good and pull your snow suit over the tops of your boots."

"I will, Mama," he replied.

Then I thought up a little challenge for Ben. "Now Ben, let's see if you can get dressed faster than I can say 'Geronimoby Dickinson shine all the time' ten times."

"Okay, but get my stuff out first before you start," he said getting ready for a little race against time.

I went to the hall closet and pulled out his coat, mittens, and boots. "Okay," I said, "Get on your mark, get set, go!" With that instruction Ben kicked into motion.

His swiftness amazed me and somewhere after starting the game, I stared at my own son with new eyes. He was changed, older. I'd always thought of him as the baby, but he wasn't a toddler any longer. His eyes looked wiser, his mouth fuller, his face so much like John's face.

All at once, his overall demeanor appeared different. He even seemed a little melancholy in the midst of his race with time. My attention was drawn to his eyebrows; they looked just like his father's.

This change in his appearance must have occurred while I was sleeping overnight. I hadn't noticed any of these traits before.

Ben had dressed so quickly that I had forgotten to start the count, so he won by default. "You win," I told him.

"Are you going to play too?" he asked hopefully.

I realized we'd done little together since John's death, but still, I declined. "It's too cold right now," I said, not thinking very sensibly.

Ben jumped up from the chair. "I've got to get outside before I fry like a fish. It's hot in here!" He raced to the door then turned back to say, "Are you sure you don't want to play Mama? It's good for your muscles." He held up his arms to show me his biceps.

I shook my head and waved him outside. Back inside the house I enjoyed a good visit with Walter. I wanted to know what he had planned for Christmas and how his daughter was doing at work. He asked me when Mother was returning to Idaho. "I don't know," I told him. I didn't know because Mother hadn't quite decided.

With that, I excused myself a moment, pulled on a jacket and stepped outside to see if Ben had turned into an icicle. Michael had most of the sidewalk done. "Hey, you two boys, how are you doing with the snow?"

Ben giggled and charged toward me for a hug, "Mama we're not boys, we're men."

"Oh, I see," I said. I wondered what Michael was thinking. He was handy with a shovel and Ben seemed to be enjoying being outdoors with one of the "men." "Ben, let me check your hands to see if they're cold."

"My hands and feet are toasty warm," Ben said with a big grin.

"And Michael, I appreciate your concern and help. When will you be going back to Texas?"

"I have to return tomorrow," he said wistfully staring off toward the roadway.

"Well, we will miss you. My boys told me last night that they had been spending quite a lot of time with you. I guess I have been in such a daze, I hadn't realized the time had slipped by without my knowing about something so important."

"Anne, I've learned several things from them," Michael said, his mustached lips turned up again into this thoughtful smile.

Ben popped into the conversation, "We showed him our rock collection and we showed him how to blow big giant bubbles with bubble gum. And he taught us how to arm wrestle."

"Sounds pretty important," I said, nodding. "I don't want you boys, I mean men, to work too hard out here. It is so fresh and clear, like a winter wonderland isn't it?"

"We don't get snow in Texas much. It is, indeed, a postcard perfect day, Anne."

"I bet you're freezing to death by now."

"To tell you the truth, Anne, it doesn't seem all that cold right now. Not with the sun shining from the sky and you radiating right here in front of me."

My ears felt hot. "Well, whether you're done with the walkway or not, you'd better get inside the house in about 15 minutes. Mother is going to assist Walter with lunch today and we'll all sit down in the kitchen to eat." I scooped up a handful of snow and threw it toward Ben.

"Hey, that's a great idea. Snowball fight!" Ben said. He gathered some snow and flung it at me hitting me on the shoulder.

"You want to fight, huh?" I ran forward, ducked behind the big sycamore tree in the front yard. A twinkle came to Michael's eyes, he scooped up some snow and packed it into a huge snowball. He threw it half-heartedly at Ben.

Ben's eyebrows shot upward. "Hey, I thought you were on my side!" Ben exclaimed.

I threw a snowball at Ben again. I hit him right on top of the head. The packed snow burst into pieces and sprinkled the ground like shattered glass.

"This means war!" Ben cried out and started making more snowballs for another round. "Michael, let's get Mama."

I hurried, made several more snowballs. It felt good to be outside in the crisp air, good to play, good to feel something. My hands were tingling with cold but I loved it. I hadn't felt anything for days. Ben was helping me cope with life whether he knew it or not. Look, frankly he hadn't forgotten how to have fun.

Michael threw a snowball at the tree I was standing behind. I peeked out to throw one at him when a snowball caught me on the neck. Snow sifted down my shirt.

I raced to the house like a shot rabbit. "I need gloves," I yelled. Meanwhile Michael and Ben were scooping up snow and stockpiling their arsenal of snowballs.

This fun made me think of my brother, Steve, when he and I were young. Back then, during winter, we would play *fox and geese* in the snow and build snow huts. In the summer we would play *army* and *shoot out at the OK Corral*, sometimes using only our fingers. We invented lots of games and we had outstanding imaginations. It was great fun. Back in the moment inside the house, I whipped on my gloves and a coat and hurried back outside.

"Wait a minute before you throw," I ran screaming. "I have to get some ammo ready." Just then a snowball hit me on the back. I turned and said, "All right, who threw that?"

Ben pointed to Michael. So he didn't want to play fair, "You better watch it, Mister," I said, "because I've got one heck of an arm for throwing. I used to be pitcher for City League Fast Pitch softball."

I wound up and threw a snowball at Michael. He ducked it. I made another snowball. I felt like a teenager again. Life seemed suddenly very exciting. I felt as though I'd finally found the world I had been seeking. I had been stranded from myself and beyond myself far too long perhaps. And the thought came to me, why was it, that in my existence with John, everything in my life had grown to be so quiet and almost alien. I didn't realize that I had become a formality in seven short years. I had achieved the height of glory in some people's eyes, but I was, in fact, like everybody else. I was ordinary, however, I had become an extraordinarily boring person weighed down by all sorts of stiff attitudes and modes of conduct. It wasn't the real me. It wasn't the old me, the natural me. And now there was snow, and throwing snowballs and this brought out the natural me! My pulse raced.

I threw three snowballs in succession finally hitting Michael twice as he dodged back and forth. Ben was lobbing snowballs toward me. I ran beside the house behind the pine tree. Ben yelled, "Charge!" Ben and Michael galloped toward me as I pelted them with snowballs. They hit me three times so I fell down in the snow to ham up a death scene. "Oh, no, you got me!" I moaned. It was fun playing dead. I groaned and writhed on the snow, making an angel-like impression in the snow.

To my surprise, Michael grabbed me by the boots and started dragging me across the snow. I was transformed into a bobsled, sliding across the mounds of snow. "Ee-haw!" he yelled. He was laughing and snorting with Ben beside him imitating his conduct. I crossed my arms over my breast in an attempt at solemn dignity. Then Michael stopped and there was a little pause of silence. I tried to lie very still.

"Let's bury her now," said Ben." He flicked some snow into my face. The white powder immediately turned to water. I felt the moisture running down my cheeks.

I lay still a bit longer, making them think that I was indeed, gone—dead. When Ben became concerned, I threw out my arms and shrieked, "You're not going to bury me." Then I jumped up and started flinging snow on them. Michael's eyebrows shot upwards. They were now frosted with snow.

Without warning, Michael grabbed me and tossed me over his shoulder, "You're our prisoner now, Anne, Queen of the Scots. Furthermore, it's time for lunch and all you get is bread crumbs with water." He tromped toward the house. Ben followed us giggling. We waited at the door and Ben opened the front door.

It felt good to be held by such powerful muscles as Michael had and it felt wonderful to smell the delicious smell that he possessed. His cologne filled the air. He was a very attractive, strong, and sweet-smelling man. He stood me down carefully holding onto my arms. A silent moment passed between us as our eyes met. My heart rose in my throat and I felt myself melting. I fluttered my eyelashes. He carefully whisked the snow from my bangs. My heart began pounding wildly. Michael was without guile and I felt as though he understood me. I blinked and broke my gaze as I suddenly looked down, then we ceremoniously tromped in the entryway. We stood there to shake off the snow from our boots.

"Mother," I called, "is it about lunch time? We're famished." My nose detected the aroma of meat roasting. It smelled delicious and I my stomach was growling.

Mother answered from the kitchen, "Oh, yes, Anne, how many am I feeding?" I believe that she was trying to encourage me to make sure Michael was staying to dine with us, not that she hadn't all ready invited him herself.

Michael, Ben, and I sauntered into the kitchen. There on the kitchen table lay a huge puzzle in process of completion. Mother and Walter were carefully piecing it together. Walter glanced up as we came into the kitchen.

"We have a treat today for lunch, kiddies," Walter said, "We are having my famous Dutch Apple Pie for dessert so make sure you save room for it. And Abigail Ross will announce what we're having for lunch before dessert." Walter took Mother's hand and she rose for the announcement.

"Well," she said clearing her throat, "we thought we'd have:

> something festive yet filling
> something hot on a cold day, yet thrilling
> and something unkosher, God willing.

"Oh, by the way, we are using the counter not the kitchen table. We still have our castle to complete." She stepped to the oven wearing large hot pad mits on both hands. She looked like a Muppet master in performance.

I could smell what was cooking before it was set out. "Sweet and sour pork, my favorite," I said savoring the smell.

"And . . ." Mother continued, "baked potatoes, a shrimp salad, and sliced green peppers and tomatoes for the festive color. We're also going to use paper plates . . . again, so much less work involved." Mother busied herself. Walter stood beside her to take the potatoes from the oven. "Walter, would you get the sour cream and chives from the refrigerator please?" Mother asked him.

"Yes, ma'am, I will. Yes indeed," he gave a low chuckle.

It wasn't long before everything was ready to eat and as we sat down, Mother cleared her throat and commented, "Are you feeling any better Anne? You seem to have some color in your cheeks today."

I simply nodded. It was the first day I'd felt truly alive. I felt as if I had some stamina. I hadn't made a serious observation of it.

"Well, you three seemed to be having the time of your life in the snow," Mother said.

"Too bad Shane wasn't here," Ben said, "he could've been on her team and helped Mama with the snowball fight."

"I must admit I did get the worst end of it this morning," I replied.

As soon as we had savored the lunch and discussed local happenings, Mother told the rest of us not to worry about the cleanup. Ben was about ready for a nap. He'd played hard all morning, so he willingly sauntered to his room. Michael and I sat in the living room with sunlight dancing off the mirror over the mantle. The light struck the two ceramic cherubs beside the clock in such a way as to make the plump angels appear to be moving.

About then we heard Mother and Walter warming up for a song duo. I heard them start to sing a song from a musical. It sounded as though they were doing their own choreographed version. What a glorious time they were having. But then the thought popped into my mind. Had they so soon forgotten about John? Had I forgotten him?

One thing that I noticed that day was that the cold weather had changed suddenly and the snow was melting away like a spring thaw. Michael stood up, and started looking at several photographs hanging on the wall. They were pictures of landscapes, family pictures, and interesting buildings.

"Anne, tell me who all these people are," he said. Who takes the pictures?" He seemed genuinely interested.

I stood up to explain. "Well, I never knew my grandparents, but this is Grandma and Grandpa Ross. This photograph was taken in Chicago in a studio setting. And this set of three are pictures of my father as a youngster. He was a handsome young man don't you think?"

"I should say, Anne. All these are good-looking people, not like some families where they are downright homely all the way through the line. Sort of like me and my family."

I jabbed at his ribs playfully. I gave him a mock serious look and said, "I can't say that you have one homely bone in your body."

He chuckled lightly.

Anne jumped in and said, "Don't get me started on ugly verses gorgeous. You don't want to hear it. Just ask Mother."

"Beauty comes from an interior life of goodness," Michael said sincerely.

"Well, sort of along those lines," I agreed. "Yes, now . . . " I continued, "This picture is of Mother when she was a youngster."

"I must say, Anne, you look a lot like your mother. You'll probably be just as stunning and captivating when you get to be her age." He raised his eyebrows. He seemed to be searching for some hint of meaning in my eyes.

I took it all in but continued without comment. "This is John and me on our wedding day. My hairstyle has change a little since then. And this is a row of yearly photos of the boys. You can see how much they've changed." I sat down in the overstuffed chair while Michael continued to stand, looking at the array of photographs sprinkled across the wall above the sofa.

"But, Anne," he said, "who took all these architectural photos, exquisite landscapes, and close-up shots of these roses?"

"Oh, I did those. I don't really classify them as anything significant."

"Well, I must say, they are absolutely exquisite," Michael said. "You capture a whole story in one shot, like a drawing an architect would make. It is truly amazing." He sat down on the sofa across from me.

I felt flattered that he had noticed my photography! There was a stretch of silence which didn't seem uncomfortable to me at all. I looked over at Michael, started telling him how sorry I felt for myself once I had the full realization that John had died. I told him how much things had changed and how I had told myself that I didn't have a life anymore.

But, as I talked, I kept twisting my wedding band around and around. Finally I jumped up from the chair and sat on the end of the sofa. My words were rambling and I was trying hard not to cry as John had advised me in the dream. But, then, there was reality to deal with. I suddenly felt like an empty well which had no life-giving water left. Yet some force was tugging at my heart. I was hoping and praying that somehow I could find new happiness and resolution of my depression.

Michael suddenly stood up, walked over, and knelt right in front of me. He took my head in his hands and tipped my head up so I was looking directly into his face. He was searching for something. The depth of his gaze was intense.

My eyes met his. I believe this was the first time I realized how truly alive I felt in the presence of this man. His response pierced my heart and the ice melted away inside. He gently took hold of my hands and held them for a few minutes. His hands felt tingly and energized upon my skin. I realized how poignant his feelings must be, how he must be thinking back to the traumatic death of his parents. I realized that he could understand me. He could comprehend the pain, sorrow, and anger I had experienced over losing my husband, I being so young and feeling so helpless. I knew it wasn't John's fault that he had died, but I had been angry with him all the same. Angry that he had left me! The message of the dream had not yet penetrated my full consciousness. However, at that moment, as Michael's voice broke into my thoughts, I was beginning to see the larger picture.

He stood up. "Anne, stand up here with me a moment." Michael pulled me to my feet. I actually discovered his face for the first time. His azure eyes were piercing. My heart was pounding, pounding. I could feel blood pulsing at my temples. He swallowed hard. Then we fell into a hug like two desperate souls clinging to life. I sobbed on Michael's shoulder trying not to think of John and my desperation without him.

Michael wept on my shoulder and muttered to me that he was thinking of the parents he lost, of the sadness of life, even of the poor desperate, misguided girl he had been tricked into marrying.

We cried, sobbed quiet tears until we had cried ourselves out. Then we sat back down side by side on the sofa. Really, it was plain that all the astronomical forces which had borne down on us with such force and without respite, had brought us to this point, it was clear we found in one another a sympathetic being to whom we could turn.

It was hard to express the fullness of that feeling without having an apprehension that there was more. It occurred to me that, perhaps, Michael did care for me in a way far beyond the wildest dreams that one should have at a time like this. And perhaps I had seen in him a solution to my life in larger terms than I wanted to acknowledge at this time. It had been so spontaneous and so quick. "Oh my," I said, and we both started to laugh through our tears.

I looked at Michael's face. It was mottled with tear stains. I'm quite sure my eyes were red as a drunkard's. However, at that moment, I did feel a great comfort, and a certain amount of honor in myself. After all, I had tried to soften the spell in which we were casting ourselves. Michael was my glimmer of hope, my small candle. Hope lit up inside me and I knew at this moment that Michael was extremely important to me, but I could not express all of this, not at such a time as this was.

Michael would not be dissuaded. He carefully smoothed down my hair which had blown about while outside. I could see splashes of tears soaking into a crisp azure area on his shirt. They were my tears.

"Thanks for stopping by," I whispered to him. I had to try to calm the situation. I squeezed his hand and moved slightly away. His hand had felt so warm and smooth. And in that gesture, I had thought perhaps light was pouring from his soul into mine, just by the touch of his fingertips. I did not tell him that. I said, "Thank you, thank you Michael." Even then I tried to sweep the feeling away, not so much like an unwanted cobweb as like an untimely realization, an unbecoming positive response and relief from grief more than I thought I should have at that moment. Finally I said, "Thank you again for everything." Then I sat silent and stared at the pattern of the carpet.

"It was nothing, Anne," he told me. At first he lowered his eyes. Next, he looked up catching my eye and said, " I would like to thank you. You must understand, this is the first time I've cried since my parents passed away. Don't misunderstand me. I know this is a time of grief for you. But I feel that I can grieve with you and that can be of some comfort to you."

I was struck with a force beyond mortal feeling. He was thanking me! I felt an electric current vibrating from my head to my toes. I was only concerned with myself and yet he needed to be comforted too in the grief, which had held in much too long.

"It was well overdue," he said. "Maybe now I can get on with my life," he said, wiping tears off his face with a white handkerchief he'd extracted from his breast pocket.

I motioned to a box of tissues near the sofa where he sat. He got it and held it up for me. Soon we were blowing our noses and making a terrible racket through the silence that prevailed. We began to laugh again. Sophie, I have to admit, that it's normal to pray to God to receive comfort, but it's also equally heartening to have a kindred soul to share a difficult moment with.

The windows of my soul had a thorough cleansing that day. It helped me see many things more clearly. I realized at that moment that all mankind born to the earth have their time and season. I needed to simplify my life by being myself. I would be a better mother to my boys. I would be a better daughter to my mother. And that's all I really needed to do at this point in my life. Discouragement at a time like this was real and I understood I could not survive without those who loved me.

I asked myself, *didn't everyone who lost a loved one, either get over it or die inside? Either believe in a higher power or be crushed by discouragement?* Maybe a ray of hope proved more solid than my physical eyes could discern. The words *carpe diem* suddenly popped into my head again. *Carpe diem*—seize the day. I realized that I needed to begin healing. I had to. This was the only day I had to live. Today! I needed to think about that and to act upon it.

Later that day Michael and I went for a walk. We poured out our dreams and fears and frustrations while walking around the neighborhood outside. We must have walked for an hour or more. It felt good to be out and about, to smell the crisp cold air, to see the blue sky peeking through the clouds. It felt good to have a friend to whom I could communicate my dreams and feelings openly, to have someone to really connect with.

Sophie, that all happened just before Christmas. And here it is still February 27. All those things happened about two months ago. Well, now I'm getting tired. As I look up at the clock, I see it is actually past midnight.

Next to my clock on the nightstand, I look over at a bouquet of dried roses. They are called *Fire and Ice*. I hadn't really noticed how intricate each petal looked even when they are dried. A whole dozen roses! Well, I must close for now. I am feeling more myself I believe. I do want to change. I know I must! I'll write more when I have time. I do want to sort out all these feelings and I do have much more to tell you. As always, Anne

MARCH 5

Dear Sophie,

How are you doing today my dear guide and wise counselor? I must say that I have been away from my writing desk, pen and ink for sufficient time to really miss being with you in spirit and talking with you. Some days, as a matter of fact, I've wondered what to do, what to be. I am here in my own tiny world, taking baby steps some days. But, to continue, here it is March fifth.

Where has the time gone? It's been over two months since Christmas, and yet, it seems as though so many things have changed with me, with my circumstances. Although I still feel as if the night darkness is deep and long, and even though fingers of despair still try to wrench the breath from my very soul, I do feel a little happier today, head up, chin up. Didn't think I'd make it at first, but now I realize I have to. I have to live for my boys and I have to live for myself. That was the message that John sent me.

Still, however, my mind turns to John's death and the anniversary of everything that marked our life together. For example: celebrating

Christmas, then celebrating New Year's Day. And, now coming right up will be Easter. Oh, yes, Easter. But, I should be recalling last Christmas and the events surrounding it—the point at which I left off last time. So I won't talk about Easter right now. To begin with, Sophie, we'll discuss how Christmas time came and passed. A time of sadness, yet a time of rejoicing. I'll try to relate what happened beginning with last Christmas Eve.

Last Christmas Eve, as I remember it, the events occurred in this fashion. After supper, there I was at home with my children and Mother. Pine scented the house. Cinnamon scented pine cones decked the mantle. Gifts of several sizes wrapped in red and white lay under the tree. Stockings were hung on the mantle, big red ones with our names emblazoned upon them in gold. I remember Ben and Shane making sure that one stocking was hung for Misty, our cat.

I remember thinking how soothing the Christmas music sounded. It enveloped the room creating a festive atmosphere. *Hark! The Herald Angels Sing* vibrated through my soul as the windows stood arrayed with tiny lights shimmering like stars. Holly garlands were wrapped around the banister and hung draped in every door frame. The main lights were off and the tiny white lights sparkled everywhere. The house seemed cheery and inviting.

Plates heaped full of homemade candy sat upon the coffee table: pink and green spearmint divinity, fudge loaded with walnuts, pecan rolls. sliced fruitcake, caramels. Traditional Christmas music continued playing on the CD player. I was feeling melancholy, yes, but more than that, I was feeling a certain amount of victimization. I grimaced, thinking of my misfortune in being a widow. I simply couldn't accept it. I was rebelling against it. I thought of the traditions we held as a family, simply being together as a family was a tradition.

And, having family visit us. How was I supposed to survive without that structure and that secure moral base?

There I was, Sophie, sitting in the living room trying to enjoy the festive atmosphere, when Mother and Father Olson stopped by to leave some gifts for all of us. John's death had been devastating to me, and of course it was devastating for them too. But they believed there was a purpose in all things and that this purpose was beyond their wishes and was in the hands of God. They truly believed in a loving God who cared for all his children. But me? Well, I couldn't see where there could be any purpose in having John taken from my life. At least I preferred to think that I couldn't. I preferred to believe that it could not lead to some better purpose that God had in store for me.

As I let them into the house, Mother Olson's salt and pepper neat coiffure glistened under the twinkling lights. Her sketched on eyebrows rose and fell punctuating each statement like an exclamation mark. "How are you feeling Anne?" she struggled with the sentence as she slipped off her gloves. "How are the boys doing?"

I told her, "I think they're doing better. I'm feeling much better. I'm glad Mother could come from Idaho to spend the holiday with us. We're getting along the best we can. I don't really think the boys realize the full extent of what has happened. I know I didn't when my father died."

And then Dad Olson spoke up. As he was beginning to speak, I took a good look at him. He was the double image of John except he had silver hair which was neatly parted on one side. I told them both to come in and sit down. Dad took hold of my hands and we walked over to the sofa. With both of my hands still in his, he sat down and pulled me to his side on the sofa.

Father Olson was trying to comfort me. "We realize that getting through the holiday season will be difficult Anne. Keep your chin up and try not to get discouraged," he then squeezed my shoulder tight as I gave a little sniff. "I'm sure John is playing in some big band now, in a grand concert hall with all the other Olson musicians."

I tried to smile. Then the Olson's fell silent. All I could hear was the hum of the electric clock.

"My, it's quiet in here. Where are the boys?" Mother Olson asked, looking about the corners of the room.

"They are downstairs with Mother and Walter," I said. "I'll call them up as soon as I tell you about a dream I had."

In this quiet moment while Mother and Walter and the two boys were playing downstairs. Mother Olson hugged me. We each dabbed at our tears with tissues. Then I told them about the dream I had about John.

When I finished, a tear slipped from Mother's eyes and she grasped my hand. Then stressing each sentence, she said, "Thank you dear, for telling us that. I'm sure John is doing fine. We all miss him not being here with us. But it's up to us to live our lives the best we can so that when we see him again . . . " I could see her lips moving.

I tried to listen, but I couldn't really concentrate on her words. A few car lights passed the house. It was time for family gatherings, stories, contemplation, and toasts of health to all. A cluster of carolers passed our house singing *Silent Night*. The carol suddenly illuminated my mind with new meaning. It was a silent night tonight. Was it a silent night when the baby Jesus was born? With birth, as I knew it, came pain and the sound of moans and outcries. I was trying desperately to understand the true divinity of my own motherhood. After all, divine birth is beyond our scientific understanding.

At this moment on Christmas Eve, I felt like screaming. I believe now that I was struggling for rebirth myself. I excused myself a moment interrupting Mother Olson's words; I stood up to call the boys. I was still nervously dabbing away at my tears.

"Boys, could you come upstairs? Grandpa and Grandma Olson are here." I tried not to let my emotions overcome me at that moment. Dad Olson stood up and firmly took hold of my hand. I'm sure he could feel the tension in my body, the way it was charging out from my fingertips. He hugged me. I broke down, pressed my head against his chest, and sobbed. That's when the boys ran upstairs.

I thought of the words from the carolers song, *Silent night, holy night . . .* my child too, would be holy—to me and to God, my angel-child whose sire was all ready in heaven and looking down on me and my babe-to-be with love and hope.

At this moment I felt frightened and anxious that I would have a baby without my husband. Mother Olson smoothed my hair, stroked it as she stood beside me trying to smile. But I did so much want this child. In fact, this time I wanted a little girl child. Recognizing my wishes for this child gave me new calm. I silently blotted more tears away.

The boys arrived, threw open their arms and gave their grandparents a hug. Shane dashed to the Christmas tree to retrieve a gift for each of our visitors. He adored them. Ben sat on Grandma Olson's lap and jabbered about his adventures in the snow during the afternoon. Shane held Grandpa's hand and sat on Grandpa's lap too.

I felt a circle of love envelope our little gathering and, in my mind, angels were singing beside us in quiet serenade. A lone flute could be heard in my head and I thought of John. His favorite song was, *What Child is This?* He loved to play it. It was as though John stood nearby playing this heavenly flute solo.

Mother and Walter soon came upstairs to say hello. Walter was becoming well-known at my house by neighbors and family members. Mother and Walter stepped into the kitchen while the last of the hugs and thoughts were voiced. We all embraced and wept one last round and then the Olson grandparents swept off into the dark night.

When they left, the clock struck 7:00 p.m. My mother and Walter returned to the front room after the folks had left. They sat on the love seat to the side telling us of their life adventures. All was calm and brighter than it had been the previous week. The star atop of the Christmas tree seemed to beckon me to a new world. "Come celebrate life," it seemed to be calling, "and seize every day." The boys came over and sat by me on the sofa. Ben sat beside me tracing lines on the palm of my hand. Shane was looking up into my face looking for signs to indicate happiness.

I sat quiet emotionally exhausted. I was ready for bed. Several times I recall blinking hard to keep my eyes open. I was glad that John's parents had come to visit, but relieved that they had left quickly. And as I sat thinking that Christmas Eve night, I tried to find some happiness, if not for me, then at least for my two boys.

With things very quiet now and a half hour or so later, we all gathered in the kitchen for our Christmas Eve dessert. Mother had baked the traditional rice custard with one raisin in it. Cinnamon and nutmeg scented the kitchen. It felt good to taste, smell, hear, and see again.

Mother finally asked, "Who has the raisin in his or her pudding tonight?" Both boys raised their hands, giggled at each other, and said in unison, "Not really."

Walter chuckled, "Maybe that wasn't a fly in my pudding." He winked at the boys. I knew he was just teasing.

The raisin was in my pudding. I wanted to leave the family in suspense as long as possible so I said nothing.

Mother picked up the gift wrapped in gold foil. "If nobody speaks up, I'll have to donate this to a local Santa." She shook the gift lightly and the room fell silent.

I finally said, "Okay, I have the raisin. That means I get the present."

The boys had played hard outside that afternoon and very soon they began yawning. But they wanted to see me open the gift before they went to bed.

At this point, I unwrapped the gift for everyone to see. An elegant looking bottle of bubble bath emerged from the wrap. I smiled. I knew that John had chosen it and wrapped it for Christmas at least a month ago. I carefully detached the ribbon and smoothed out the wrapping paper. I meticulously peeled off the tape. I wanted to forever hold dear the paper and ribbon my dear husband had touched. Oh how I wished that John could be here again.

The boys began to wonder when they could go to bed. Shane suddenly announced, "We need to leave some carrots out for the reindeer and some chocolate chip cookies for Saint Nick."

Walter joined in the festive announcements, "I believe that your grandmother made some cookies today for this very occasion. Let's go get them." He stood up taking both boys by the hand and sauntered to the kitchen. "Yes, indeed. Let's go see what we can find in the kitchen."

Ben soon returned with three carrots and Shane followed along behind him carrying a very large plate of cookies. Walter brought a glass of milk. Mother wrote a brief note to St. Nicholas that was to be left on the table for him, along with his cookies and milk.

Now I thought at that moment, a little magic sometimes made life easier to bear. I always have believed in magical things. Over the years, I have learned that the most powerful magic stems from an individual's imagination and spirit of love and sharing. And such positive creative imagination is always very good magic.

After the cookies, carrots, milk, and note had been placed carefully on the table in the living room, we all sat down there—to be together for a short time. We did this every year. We would read together as a family, the traditional story from the Bible as found in Saint Luke, the account of the birth of the Holy Child, the Son of God. Walter read it dramatically.

Later that night after we shared these ideas and stories, I tucked the boys in bed and bid my mother and Walter goodnight. "Walter, you'd better get home so my mother can get her beauty sleep," I said. "Would you help me bring those dressers in right now. I do believe I need more beauty sleep than she does. I'm exhausted."

"You bet! I'll give you a hand." He adjusted his spectacles. "If we take the drawers out it won't be so heavy. You shouldn't be lifting too much weight around."

"I know," I said, "but I do have pretty strong muscles and we don't have far to carry the dressers."

Walter was such a big help. We talked a bit while Mother stepped out of the room to check on the boys. She wanted to make sure they were asleep. I took this opportunity to talk, "So, Walter, how do you like my mother?" I really hadn't asked before and I wanted to know.

"I believe that is kind of a personal question," Walter said. He raised his bushy eyebrows. "But, I will tell you this, Abigail is an angel." His face was suddenly more animated, "She's everything I could dream of. Yes indeed." For a moment he stared off into the corner thinking. Then he said, "Do you think she'd ever marry an old fellow like me?"

"I would say your chances are better than anybody else's."

He tapped his fingers on the nearby cabinet and nodded. He was deep in thought.

Men were different; they did not think like women. I figured that men were just happy simply to be loved. But for a woman like me, I wanted examples of love, demonstrations of love, and I needed to be told every day that I was appreciated. It takes that type of action for a man and woman to live together in a state of happiness. Walter needed only the reassurance of being told that he was loved. I implied that by my answer and I looked at him very seriously and I knew that was sufficient information for me to pass on to him.

A moment after that, I brought out a few wrapped gifts and placed them under the tree. I had a question on my mind, "Walter, did Michael get home safely?"

Walter looked up with great interest, "He did. I had wanted him to stay until the New Year. But, I'm not sure what his plans are. I believe he was going to spend Christmas day with my son." Walter fell into thinking again. There was a silent pause. Then he continued, "Oh, by the way, Michael wanted me to bring over the gifts he got for you and the boys. By golly, I nearly forgot about them."

"Oh my," I said, "he didn't need to get us anything." My pulse raced all of a sudden. I could hear my heart pounding. I was somewhat startled that Michael would think of us. It was deeply touching to my soul.

Walter was making comment to my last statement, "Well, that's just the way he is, he was really taken with Shane, Ben, and . . ." Walter didn't finish his sentence. He looked into my eyes, scratched his head. "Yes indeed, I'll bring those gifts in from my pickup before I forget about them." He shook his head as he scooted toward the doorway.

As he closed the front door, I stood there wondering what the gifts would be. I felt like a child who could not sleep wondering over what gift I had been sent. Walter made two trips to the truck. Two good sized boxes that were identical he carried into the house first and a larger box was his second bundle. The large rectangular box bearing a large red ribbon had my name carefully handwritten on a card attached to it. I wanted to open it then and there. But I knew I must wait for Christmas. I bit my lip with apprehension. What could be in that large box?

But we went on with our chores. Soon Walter and I had both dressers in the living room. He slid all the drawers in place and I tied a big red ribbon around them with a sign saying "From your Mother and Father." Mother reappeared about then, so I told Mother and Walter *goodnight* again, gave them both a hug and retired to my bedroom.

It felt so good to have my very own mother in the house. I was her little girl. She made me feel safe and secure. And Walter certainly proved to be a treasure beyond imagining. After Walter left the house and my mother had turned out the lights, I was still staring at my ceiling.

I didn't know if I could possibly sleep after pulling on my flannel nightgown, saying my prayers, and climbing into bed. There were so many ideas swirling in my mind: presents, Christmas, John, and Walter. I finally drifted into dreamland.

The ideas I had thought about as I fell asleep now reappeared in my dreams. And there was Michael in my dreams. He was waltzing with a stylish woman. When the dance ended, he kissed the woman. I couldn't see her face and I wondered desperately who she was. Did I have some aspiration regarding Michael and this woman in my dream? I wasn't sure. But one thing I knew, in my dream, *Oscar de la Renta* cologne and leather scents filled the air in the room where Michael and the woman kissed in my dream.

Some time near midnight I had finally drifted into deep slumber, when suddenly something startled me. I heard a noise in the living room. We'd never had burglars before. I jumped out of bed and carefully peeked out into the hallway.

The light from the street partially lit the living room. I looked back into my bedroom at my digital clock which read 4:15 a.m. I walked down the hall tripping on something in the hallway. I caught myself and peered carefully around the corner. I didn't see St. Nick! But I did see two boys—my boys! And they each held a flashlight lighting up objects in the room.

Shane was quietly but earnestly scolding Ben for something, "You dummy," Shane said, "why did you loop that string around the door and down the hall for me to trip on?"

"Well, I wanted to get Saint Nick's attention," Ben said. "I waited till I heard Mama close her door. Then I rigged it up after Walter left and after Grandma went downstairs."

Shane flashed his light around. He was flashing the beam of light on the tree, on the presents, on the ceiling. "How are we going to sneak in here and look at our presents if you go catching St. Nick like an old skunk?"

"I didn't know you were getting up. I would have told you about my trap," Ben said. His tone sounded indignant.

"It looks like Santa has all ready come," Shane said. "I'm glad you didn't catch him. He could have knocked himself out on the hearth," Shane was disgusted. He was scolding away.

"Well he just got away without a sound. I didn't even hear him," Ben said in a tone both disappointed and disgruntled.

"Wow, look at this! It has my name on it," Shane said. "What's this big tall thing here, there's two of them."

"Oh that's our dressers that Walter made."

"Really, they're for us? He really made them? Well, yippie!" Shane gave a hearty yell that could have raised the hair on the hides of Santa's reindeer.

"Pipe down or you'll wake Mama and Gram up," Ben said.

I was on the verge of giggling aloud over the antics of these two little adventurers in the night. But I didn't want them to know that I had seen them. It was their secret. I watched them in guarded silence.

Shane looked at the plate of cookies, "Hey, all the cookies are gone."

"No carrots," Ben said. "Wow, Santa and his reindeer ate them all up. He really came. I knew he would come!"

They dug through the gifts like two miners seeking gold. They surveyed everything in the room and I knew exactly which presents they would claim come morning.

I quietly slipped into my bedroom trying not to catch my foot in the string that was placed down the hall. I carefully closed my door behind me, slipped to my bedside and climbed into bed. I curled up like a kitten trying to get completely comfortable. It had been entertaining to see the boys so thrilled about the magic of Christmas. I tried to be happy and not to cry myself to sleep. I had too many things racing around in my brain and I was wide awake by this time.

I decided to play a little game in my mind. I forced my thoughts back to the happiest Christmas I ever had. I was going back to a perfect past. My thoughts flew backward in time until I remembered a particular Christmas day when I was much younger.

I must have only been eight or nine the Christmas I had gotten my first camera. I remember the prancing reindeer wrapping paper that concealed my treasure. A big red and white bow nearly as large as the package sat carefully perched on top.

The camera was a dream come true. After opening my gifts that day, I dressed for cold weather and ran outside. I had taken pictures of everything. I took pictures of family members, our dog, the trees, snow, our house. I was crazy about my brand new camera.

Later when my first roll of film hadn't developed any pictures, I felt deflated, crushed. I guess the film hadn't rolled correctly somehow. A week later, I was even more voracious with the next roll of film. I had hoped the film would turn out and this one had. Some of the pictures had a thumb hiding the main subject, the camera strap obscured others. But I felt invigorated and free to express ideas from a child's point of view. Of course that was years ago. As I focused back on the present, I thought of my camera in the here and now.

I still felt that way whenever I had a camera in my hands. It had become an obsession. Recently I'd tried to cut back to a roll or two a month. But lately, I wondered, who would want any of these old photos when I become an old dead ancestor? Most of the pictures weren't labeled and many old college acquaintances had become nameless faces.

My thoughts returned to Ben and Shane. I wondered what they would do without a father.

I had been so amused by their antics. I was so delighted they were having the time of their lives, that I had not thought of the hardship that waited before them. Then again, I wanted to have the time of my life too. I was fed up with death, sorrow, and crying myself inside out. I felt it had to cease that very instant. I had done pretty well since the dream about John. I had believed that I couldn't imagine my life without John, but here I was on my own again and doing fairly well. I had to get on with my life. Death had slithered into the scene in the past but death was not going to beat me. I would win. I would survive somehow. I was thinking, along those lines. I knew that I had to have some positive reinforcement in my life or I would go mad.

But what was it that I had to forget? What did I want to forget? I wanted to forget that I took John for granted, that I took life for granted, that I took my life for granted! I thought everything would simply continue forever along a timeline perfectly. Now I had to have the last great question resolved. What was to come next? What if I were to die? What would my boys do? I was forced to think along serious lines. I could not be passive any longer. I decided that I had to find a way to celebrate life each day!

I realized that I needed to make some changes in my life. I needed to slow down and evaluate my life, plot out a direction for my life and dreams and set certain goals. You see, Sophie, I needed to live each day in simple celebration of my soul and body, the breathing in and out every day. I had two boys, I needed to raise them. I needed that constant whispering in my mind, in my soul which said, "Love your boys, spend time with them, raise them the proper way. Do it for John, do it for yourself, do it for the spiritual marriage that you had with John and for your belief in the spiritual purposes of marriage."

This was a turning point. I realized at that moment that I couldn't give in to the fear, disappointment and upheaval that wastes many good people when they lose their partner in life. I wasn't dead yet. I had to stand up and fight as long as my heart beat within me.

So, Sophie, do you see? Can you understand that this point in my life became the phase of "get on your mark, get set, go?" I heard imaginary gun fire. I was beginning the main track event of my existence. I didn't know it then, but I'm beginning to see it now. I knew I would never forget John. A part of him would ever be in my heart to spark hope, and light, and the courage to go on. I accepted the fact that it would take a good year to learn to live fully, without feeling that I was showing disrespect to John's memory. The anniversary of everything John and I had done together in the past year would continue to mark my life.

Just a couple of days ago, as a matter of fact, I was thinking of some of the people who had influenced my life. People who had helped make me who I am. They include: Mother; Dad; my sisters; Steve and John; my teachers in school at all levels of learning; Mother Teresa; the Apostle James; the homeless beggars sitting on corners in downtown Salt Lake City; Benjamin Franklin; Jesus Christ; Charles Dickens; Renoir, John Keats. You see, it is not only the people who are living now, but those who have died. I have read about their lives. I have read their works. I have felt them breathing next to me by seeing their creations. Their lives have touched me and they, too, are a real part of my life.

I'll never forget a horse-shoe man at Rockford, my father, a man gentle with the stock even as he pounded nails into their hooves. I can't forget Thomas Jefferson, Lewis and Clark, Michelangelo. Wolfgang A. Mozart, Bach, Handel, Dad and Mother Olson, Mrs. Cunningham, Shane, Ben, Walter, and now Michael.

And, Sophie, you have changed my life too. I'm sure everyone could list one person who has been a good influence in his or her life. Everyone is happier when he or she can realize that another human being has helped one to grow through caring, love, and simple acts of kindness.

Believe me, Sophie, I grew up in a home where marriage meant commitment and loyalty. Marriage had a purpose. It was important. And although I have complained in the past about John's short comings, I believe he was a good husband. He was a good, honest man who provided for his family. The problem we had is that neither one of us tried to develop the spiritual relationship and aspects of our marriage. We were concerned with the physical, ethical, social and moral aspects of our marriage, but we were not introspective. We did not really think of the spiritual inner life. We concentrated on the roles we had to play, on doing our daily duty, on teaching the letter of the moral law to our children. These things are all good and important—but they are merely the basics of building a spiritual marriage.

The true spiritual marriage strives for understanding of the Christly aspects of the relationship. The meditation on the meaning of love and parenthood. The prayers for greater sensitivity to the character of eternal life. The conversations about true inner peace, true piety, true charity, true faith in the message of God and the individual relationship with God and the Saints. The spiritual marriage leads each partner to aid in the salvation and beautification of the other partner. The spiritually married do not live a selfish existence concentrating only on the material well-being of the partners immediate family members. A spiritual marriage is given to study and sharing of the truths of philosophy, art, history, music, poetry as these art studies are dedicated to the glorification of God and goodness. Marriage should be one of the greatest ways to grow spiritually—not an excuse for living from day to day, holding on to the practical, over-feeding the physical, self-satisfaction or self-indulgence.

This was the way in which John and I did not reach high enough, try hard enough to live heavenly lives on earth. For all my life, I did not understand this until now.

Where has the time gone? I really must close for now, dear Sophie.

As always Anne

APRIL 18

Dear Sophie,

Over a month has passed and it is already mid-April. I have had a lot of things going on and haven't had a chance to take up my pen. But sitting here in the kitchen I now pen a few lines. We had a cold spell move through yesterday but today, although it's cold and wet, the sun peeped out this morning. With the sunshine, I feel full of hope. I even put on some makeup this morning. Yesterday I bought a pair of earrings with two solid gold hearts. I'm told they really set off my smile. The store clerk said so. But, anyway, I'm smiling again. I'm trying to take one day at a time. I'm breathing in and breathing out.

Two days ago, I took the boys over to Mrs. Cunningham's. I went out and took some photographs in the area. I didn't realize there were so many interesting things in the vicinity. I drove over to the old brick kilns and took some fascinating shots from inside looking out. These are the old kilns that some of the Olson's helped build around the early 1850's so the settlers could fire their own bricks and build solid houses in their newly established town. John used to talk about them, but I'd never actually been out to the kilns to look at them.

I also took some interesting photo shots of houses, of old buildings and structures. There's this house on Pine Canyon road that is stained wood. I asked the residents if I could take a few pictures of their house. They were delighted. I also drove up the old Smelter Road for a better shot of the lake, took my telephoto along. I felt exhilarated being out with my camera.

But I realize that in my excitement, I haven't told you what actually transpired on Christmas. So now going back to last December, you'll never believe what happened and what's happening even as I write this. I'm thrilled, absolutely convinced that life will go on for me and go on in a very happy state. Well, let me begin my story anew.

Christmas Day. The actual appearance of the sun was a good hour in coming. Inside the house, darkness enveloped everything. The furnace kicked on and the clock on the wall tick-tocked. Inside the front room a few strands of light from the outside yard lights sliced through a small parting in the drapes.

Outside, fresh snow lay on the ground and covered the house and yard. Everything had a kind of insulated, protected sense. The wind had died out during the night and stillness enwrapped the Tooele valley. I could only think, this is Christmas Day! The day when Christians celebrate the birthday of Jesus Christ.

As I lay in my bed I thought of what would transpire. Soon the day would be thrown into a furious grinding of gears and the roar of celebrating by gift giving, eating, and relaxing. As I lay thinking I suddenly heard footsteps in the hallway.

Ben dashed to my bedside with a flashlight beaming and announced, "It's time to get up and open presents." This looked to me like a scene out of a Batman movie.

"Could you get that out of my eyes please?" I pushed the flashlight so the beam was on the ceiling. "We have to eat our breakfast first. Get out of your pajamas and into your play clothes."

Shane bounced in. "Ah, do we have to?" he asked. "I want to open my presents."

"You too, Sir Shane. Get those pajamas off and into your play clothes."

"I'll go get Gram up," Ben chortled, wiggling like a puppy out of control.

"Have you looked at the gifts?" I asked.

"Oh, Mama, we have dressers to put all our stuff in!" Shane said with wide eyes. He started listing all the things he could put in his fine new dresser. I let him go on with his list. I just wanted to roll over and resume peaceful slumber.

"What time is it?" I asked interrupting the boys canting. I glanced at the digital clock which read shortly after 7:00 a.m. I answered my own question, "Past 7:00 a.m.? You boys are up late. Listen, I'll make French toast. After breakfast we'll open our gifts."

"Is Walter coming over today?" Shane asked.

"I'm planning on it."

"Did we get anything for him?" asked Ben.

"Of course we did. It's under the tree in the big red and silver wrap." I thought about the gifts that Michael had sent to me and the boys. I got out of bed, threw on my robe anxious to find out what those wrapped boxes contained.

The boys ran into the living room shouting Christmas "Ho! Ho! Ho!" They wanted to verify my words. They looked for Walter's package.

Seeing this I contemplated the glorious event that was happening before my eyes. Two strong, healthy boys! It was a joy to watch them bustle about in such a holiday mood. There was no day like Christmas. And there was no time like now to seize upon the fact that life was in full swing with two energetic boys around.

I walked down the hall, started feeling a little melancholy. I was thinking that John should be there. I walked into the kitchen. Santa may have found my house, but Mr. Sandman certainly hadn't. There were so many things with which I had to concern myself that I wondered if I could possibly have a merry Christmas.

Ben followed me to the kitchen. He wanted to help with breakfast. "Good," I told him and soon we had sizzling sausages, hot cocoa, and French toast aroma filling the kitchen. It was enough to wake up all the senses.

Shane joined us and set the table. Mother bounced in wearing her powder blue bath robe. She came in and helped pour hot cocoa in our cups. She noticed how Shane had set the table including a place for his daddy. When everything was near ready I told everyone, "Let's all gather round, have a prayer and eat."

Now, Sophie, as soon as we had a blessing on the food, I began eating my French toast. All of a sudden, there came an insistent rapping on the front door. Then the doorbell rang three times in rapid succession. I dabbed my mouth with a table napkin and stepped to the door. I couldn't imagine what was going on. It was very strange for someone to be at my home at such an hour on Christmas Day.

I turned on the porch light and saw a young couple standing there. I opened the door but wasn't about to unlock the screen. I couldn't make out their features. The girl was sporting a parka and had long black hair cascading out of a matching hat. The young man had a familiar look about him, but he wore a cold scowl with a chin full of stubble, and he had long mustang-like mane sticking out wildly at his shoulders.

"What do you want?" I said trying to become more acquainted with their features. "What are you doing here? This is Christmas!"

The man was intent upon entering the house. My mother stepped to the door, half scowling herself—but searching out the features of the people. As she got closer and closer to the doorway, she cried out, "Oh, dear Lord. My Steven!"

There was a furor at the screen as Mother's fingers became nimble enough to unlock the screen latch. She fell into the arms of this man. I was in a state of shock. I could barely comprehend. Then it struck me, Steven was NOT dead! Of course not. We'd always hoped that he was not dead. My brother had returned. Oh, holy day! Oh, happy day! Oh magnificent unbelievable, marvelous day!

I ran onto the porch to hugged Mother, hugged Steven. I nearly knocked them down in my excitement. Tears erupted, they ran down my face. They were crying. I was crying. I couldn't express myself enough. I couldn't say, "Oh, dear God, thank-you" enough. I couldn't cry out the magic of the day, the holiness of it all! Sophie, you cannot imagine what a Christmas gift this was. It was more than the gift of the Magi. It was magnificent. I cried and cried. I couldn't stop crying. I had to touch Steve's face, his arms. I felt his eyelids. It was my brother. "Steven! You've come back! You've come back!" I said. "Oh praise be to God." I hugged him in gratitude. He was the realization of every hope that I had ever had. Oh, I had my brother back again. Joyous day!!

"Let's get inside the house before we all freeze," Mother said. "Oh, my dear! We heard you were murdered, but we never gave up hope. We always hoped . . . believed. We always hoped that you were all right!"

There were many telling minutes. All we could do was thank God and try to touch Steven. Together again. My boys ran forward to be with us. They hadn't seen Steven for a long time and they had no idea who this stranger could be. But it was a glorious moment for me. We hugged and kissed more inside while the young lady stood nearby. Everyone was hugging and kissing. We were exhausting ourselves with expression, with wordless delight, with appreciation and thanks to God.

An hour later, we were sitting more calmly in the living room. Mother was speaking to Steven, "Dear Steven! My only son! You know, they told us you were murdered in Bolivia. Not that I believed it as I said before."

Steven drew his eyebrows together." Well, they were wrong Mother." He could hardly contain himself. He was so delighted to be able to give this news to Mother.

"And you're the same strong man you ever were, six feet tall and what do you weigh now my son?"

"I weigh about 160 pounds, Mother. And I guess that for me is a little on the gaunt side.

But I haven't lost a thing. I've remained strong and fairly healthy," Steven said. He glanced at Mother's face, "Oh, *Mamacita*, you're looking so beautiful. I'm so thrilled to see you. How sorry I am that it took over two years for me to get back home. There were many adventures. I was in prison for a time. I had to travel by night. I had to move through the dark for one whole year I couldn't leave one whole village where I was entrapped. There was no way to communicate, no way I could explain what had happened. Otherwise I would have relieved your suffering immediately. I would have come back immediately. But, it was impossible. All the political ramifications, all the demands of the army intelligence service. And then they had to bring me back and debrief me. They didn't allow me to contact any family members. It was a nightmare, years in the making. But, at last, I did have permission, so long as I arrived without creating any scene. And here I am."

Mother let out a little squeal, "You're so bright," she said, "and so strong and so handsome and so fine. I knew that God would send you back to me. I knew it. I knew it. I knew it!" Mother could hardly stop saying those words to Steven she was so overjoyed to see him.

Then Steve said, "Mother, I want to introduce you to someone." He pointed to the young lady who had remained sitting off to the side. She had not rushed forward when all of the family did. "Mother I want you to meet Angelique. She saved my life or most likely I would still be in Bolivia. And every step of the way, she has been my companion. She is a very special person to me and I'm sure she will be to you."

Mother looked over toward the young lady. Her arm still around Steven, "I'm very glad to meet you. I thank you for all that you have done for my son. We want you to know how much we appreciate your kindness. We love Steven and we are so glad he is home."

"I'm so glad I finally got to meet you," Angelique said, "Steven has talked so much about all of you." There was a slight silence. Then Angelique said she wanted to explain her position. "I know how parents worry when their children are away. I have tried to keep in touch with my mother and my father, so they wouldn't be concerned about me. It was a dangerous time and area for Christians as well as Americans.

"When I met Steven, I found him to be responsible, secure! Knew that he would help protect me. I had tried to help at the Catholic missions. One time I had to hide with the nuns so I would not be detected by those who would seek my destruction. At one point I contacted my priest to try to secure help for Steven and two other Americans helping him in his operation." She paused a moment and looked over at Mother and then back to Steven.

Steve got up from the sofa and walked over to the kitchen table where the two boys, perched on their chairs, watched wide-eyed. I suppose Shane and Ben wondered who Steven really was. It hadn't been explained. Perhaps they thought he was St. Nicholas. *What was the meaning of Steven?* They most likely were wondering, *Why was Grandmother so excited? Why was their mother so excited?*

I hadn't stopped to explain in the flurry of events. I hadn't told them much about Steven, not that they hadn't heard some talk, but it had not sunk in. They had not comprehended it. At that moment Mother walked up to Steven and threw her arms around him. She was proclaiming the she would never again let him out of her sight.

With that statement, Steve embrace her again, replied," Well, well, beautiful *Mamacita*, don't cry! You know John and I are tough, we'll never die."

Now, true darkness fell over the room.

I bit my lip. I didn't want to ruin the holiday mood. I wiped a few tears from my eyes, but the tears continued, then they spilled over. Steve certainly didn't know. It was Steve that we thought was gone. And Steve had no idea that his best friend, my husband, John, was gone.

Mother looked at me and then back at Steve. "Oh Steven," she was very somber and sober in her tone, "Come sit down you two. Angelique, Steven, come sit with me." She took Steven and Angelique by the hand and led them to the sofa.

I took their wraps and coats. I knelt in front of Steve gripping his hands while Mother sat closely beside him on the sofa.

Mother licked her parched lips and cleared her throat. Her eyes were moist. "Steven, I don't know what we can tell you. We've had so much that has happened here."

Steve wrinkled his forehead. His brown eyes were upon her. He took Angelique's hand. "What kind of problems?" he asked. "By the way, where is Johnny?" He began glancing around the room.

I held tighter to Steve's hands. Mother gripped our hands with hers. "Oh, dear Steven," Mother said, "the Lord has brought you home to us! But the Lord has taken our Johnny away!"

"What are you talking about?" Steven muttered, "Took him where?"

"Steve, John is gone. He has died," I replied. My lips were trembling. I couldn't think of anything more difficult to announce. I said the final words. There, they spilled out, but I hated to have to tell Steven this news.

"What are you saying?" Steven stood up, "You're not making any sense."

"I'm afraid it is a fact," Mother stated plainly, "John is gone."

"No, no, not Johnny! What happened?" Steven's eyes suddenly burst with tears.

Mother told him briefly of the events. She explained the accident. She explained also that John had a condition, a loss of balance.

"Johnny really went out in a blaze. Dear Lord! Mother, are you sure?"

Mother affirmed his question with a nod.

Steve broke down in Mother's arms. Presently he sobbed like an abandoned child.

The boys poked in their heads. Ben was crying. Well, both boys were crying. They understood that everyone was crying about their daddy whom they now really had come to miss. I looked around; I noticed that even Angelique was wiping her eyes. I cried again.

After we cried, I asked Steve and Angelique if they had eaten breakfast. They explained that they had gotten a bite at the Salt Lake City Airport before driving straight to Tooele. So they truly had not eaten. But they were in a hurry. They had wanted to surprise me and Mother for Christmas. Steve had figured Mother would be at my house. Everything else fell into place.

Listening to all this, I had time to reflect further upon the relationship between John and Steve. They were more like brothers than brother-in-laws. John and Steve had hunted deer together; they had attended U of U games in Salt Lake during basketball and baseball season. And now Steven was back, but John was not.

Steve was crushed by the news and I was greatly affected by his realization of the matter. My dear brother Steven! He had always been such a soft-hearted, true person. When we were growing up in Illinois, Steve, Jo, and I had compared ourselves to the Three Little Pigs—one day we all went out to seek our fortunes. Jo had become involved as a dance instructor. I did my photography and Steven had gone into the army to become part of an intelligence program.

But, still, the way we were then, we had a total commitment to one another and that had never died and would never die. We had always been connected by an invisible unbroken bond.

With Steve, we often knew little or nothing about his activities. He was two years my senior and we did many things together growing up. But the separation had been deeply felt and it was a serious one. I eyed his long unkempt hair. He must have been in a very dangerous and desperate situation in Bolivia.

While Steve would travel to all these places around the world, he never tired of telling us adventures from exotic places. We were his finest audience. He'd been to the rain forests of Brazil, the Amazon Congo, India, Saudi Arabia, France, and Italy. I'd only read about these places. My world took in Tooele and some of Northern Utah, Idaho, and Illinois.

But now, back to Christmas morning. There, as we were gathered in the living room, I remembered sounding a great sigh of relief. It was a sigh most audible. "I am spent, exhausted!" I said. "I would really like to rest a moment. Can we all go back to bed a while?"

Ben and Shane gave a hearty, "No! Let's open our presents."

"Let's finish breakfast," I said. "How about some hot cocoa for the midnight travelers?"

Angelique said, "Thank you very much. I really appreciate your kindness."

Steve's eyes were still red. He took Angelique by the hand as they stepped to the kitchen. Eyes swept to John's chair at the head of the table. John's table setting was neatly in place with a plate, silverware, and glass. There were three Hershey kisses on John's plate. I had put them there. They were encircled by a holly wreath.

Steve walked over to the table and touched the back of John's chair, his eyes full of tears again. One of Steve's tears fell on the edge of a fork in the place setting. Steve carefully wiped it dry with his fingers. He looked over at me. The room was silent except for the muted sound of our breathing. In and out. In and out. I could hear snowflakes bumping into the kitchen window. Steve suddenly moved toward me, thinking now of my pain and grief. He grabbed my hand and squeezed it tightly as he thought of my pain, "Sis, are you going to be okay?"

Holding out a cup of hot cocoa to him, I said, "Are you going to be okay?"

His hand was trembling. I set the cup down at John's place setting. "Sit here," I told him. I retired John's plate to the counter while Mother took from the microwave a cup of steaming hot cocoa. This she delivered to Angelique.

Mother sat down on one side of Steve, Angelique on the other side. Mother said, "Steve, I must tell you. Annie had a dream shortly after Johnny died. John told her that he was all right and he didn't want her to keep crying over him."

I looked at Steve to see how he was receiving this news. Mother continued, "It's okay whatever you're feeling. We all really miss him, especially now at Christmas."

Steve pressed his forehead with his fingers—as if he were smoothing away the wrinkles of distress. He sniffled, "I do have some good news, a truly joyous announcement. Mother, family. Angelique and I are getting married. We've already set the date."

"Oh, that is wonderful," Mother and I said in unison.

Let me add that I was delighted. I could tell by everything that had been said that Angelique was a marvelous woman and the right type for my brother to marry. She really cared about him.

I could tell too, that Mother felt as I did about Angelique. Mother could be cold and remote if something displeased her. And I could tell that Angelique pleased her.

Shane came over and tapped Angelique on the arm. "Are you going to be my aunt?"

"I guess so, and you'll be my nephew," Angelique said.

"Yes, I will," Shane answered.

Steve pulled Shane onto his lap, "My old pal, Shane. I don't think you remember when I used to come over here, but I know your Mama real well. She's my sister. Now, I've asked this lady standing next to me to be my wife. And she has accepted that offer. So that will make her your aunt. I gave her a substantial ring and we sealed our agreement with a kiss.

"A kiss? Oh, yuck," Shane said.

Steve was amused. He rolled his eyes. "Well sir, one day you'll fall in love with a lady and you'll seal it with a kiss too?"

"Puh," Shane puffed out his cheeks, rolled his eyes. "I'm not going to kiss Marjean Jones. Boy, she's got a case on me!"

This was news to all of us. We broke into laugher.

"Oh, I see," Steve said. "Well, you're still a little young to get married. Maybe you ought to tell Marjean she'll just have to get in line."

Shane pointed his index finger at Steve. He was very serious. "I HAVE told her."

We burst into laughter again, this time wiping tears not of grief but of laughter from our eyes.

Thereafter, I told Angelique if she needed anything she should simply ask. And then, I added, "Oh by the way, I don't think we had a minute to introduce ourselves. I'm Anne Olson and this is Mother Ross" I was then ready to deliver some news, "soon, to be Mrs. Wellington."

"What do you mean Mrs. Wellington?" Steve asked Mother.

Mother beamed, held up her hand to show off her ring. A ring Walter gave her! A ring even I didn't know about until that moment! I had been teasing—but Mother was serious.

What glorious news!

Now, Mother was ready to say more. She said, "Oh yes, Walter Wellington, a local carpenter, slash lover, gave me this ring last night. He also asked me if I would marry him."

Mother showed the ring. It was a dazzling large diamond studded with six rubies.

My mouth was agape. What an impressive ring! I was excited for Mother! I was thrilled! I was going to have a father again!

Steve whistled, "Knock my eyes out! Wow, Angelique is going to be jealous."

"I take it Anne didn't know about this?" Steven addressed the comment to Mother.

"It was a great surprise," Mother said. "Walter asked me just last night. And I accepted his proposal. We agreed to get married in May or June. Can you believe it?" She paused, looked at Steven, "Now what day have you set for your marriage?

"Well," Steve said, "we had thought about April 25 since that is your birthday."

"But, how are we going to plan two weddings so close together?" Mother wondered aloud. "Hmm, sounds like a lot of work."

Angelique spoke up, "What about a double wedding?" She walked up to Mother and inspected the ring. "It is magnificent!"

Steve put on his news commentator voice, "Ladies and gentleman out there in TV land, have I gotten all this correct? Is this enough of a shocker for the day or what! First, Johnny's not coming back. Second, Mother is engaged to a man I don't even know. And, last of all, I am getting married before summer." There was a slight pause as he surveyed his audience. "People, is there anything else I need to know? We will announce it before the next commercial break."

I knew the boys really wanted to open their gifts, but, since we were in the sharing mood, I had a little news I wanted to share with the family. I blurted it out. "I'm going to have John's baby come this summer."

Everyone fell silent. I had hoped the news would bring some happiness to the family. But what happened seemed to be another rush of unbelievable concern. Once mother realized the full implications of my statement, the fact of my having a baby and having no father to raise the child she fell mute. Steven coming home and announcing that he was getting married had been enough. The latest news was more than my poor, dear mother could bear. Suddenly she cried out, "Oh, Dear Lord," and slumped to the floor in a faint.

When Mother fell to the floor we were all surprised. Quickly we all gathered around her, Steve scooped her into his arms and carried her to my bed. All of us crowded into the bedroom with Mother on the bed lying pale.

As my brother stood up straighter, rolling his eyes. "I take it she didn't know," he said, sweat beads springing up at his temples.

I raised my eyebrows. "John and I are the only ones who knew. Oh, Secret Agent Man." Angelique and Steve both looked at me then they each hugged me. Steve told me I'd better lie down next to Mother on the bed. I complied since I was also near to faint. "I have some smelling salts in the first aid kit in the bathroom cabinet," I told Steve. He left to get the first aid kit in Mother's behalf.

The boys had been sorting presents, but suddenly in the furor, they had popped into the bedroom. Ben tugged at his ear, asked, "Is Grandma dead?"

I sat up, "No honey, she's not. She didn't pass away. She passed out."

"Well, she better not be," Ben said matter-of-factly, "'cause St. Nick brought her a big present. Are you coming to open presents?"

"Why don't you put on some nice Christmas music," I told Shane. "We'll come as soon as Grandma revives." I saw Steve heading back toward the bedroom.

With Steve back with smelling salts, he popped one vial open, waved it under Mother's nose carefully.

"What a Christmas," Angelique remarked. "Is your mother going to be all right?"

Mother soon roused from her faint. She fluttered her eyes, tried to get her bearings as she realized I was lying on the bed next to her. She cleared her throat, lying still, and said, "Oh Anne, why didn't you tell me?"

"I just couldn't after John . . . d-died." I had said the d-word again but it was still hard to hear my own voice saying it. I had finally realized the full extent of it and this overwhelmed me. "I've never told anyone about being pregnant at least not until I'm three or four months along. I think it is bad luck. Miscarriages happen sometimes, you know."

"Oh, my darling Anne. You've been so brave." Mother sat up, cleared her throat, then carefully swept the hair out of my eyes.

"I don't want to cry anymore," I said, sitting up, biting my lip. "Today is Christmas. Let's celebrate life and love, love for what we have now: Steven and Angelique, you and Walter, me and the boys. So, let's go open some presents right now."

"I brought a few things," Steve said. "They're out in our rental car. I'll bring them in." He looked at Angelique, "Come help me." They clasped hands, escaped outside with Steve shaking his head.

"Come on, Mother," I told Mother. I took her by the hand and helped her off the bed. "Do you feel well enough to get up? Do you think you can walk?"

Mother cleared her throat. "Well, I can walk," she said. "So, I think I'll be all right. Let's see what the boys are up to."

Well, dear Sophie, that day proved to be a highlight in my life. My brother Steven was home. Walter got a new carpenter's apron for his tools from us. Mother got him a warm Afghan. Santa had brought Mother a large bedroom lamp with hand painted roses. She'd always wanted one. Michael had given the boys each a Tonka truck. And he had given me an original blueprint design of a very fine house with the saying, "Home is where the heart is."

I would never forget the feeling of love and warmth that permeated our house that day. Steve had returned from the dead, living and breathing and loving. John wanted me to be happy. Mother was getting married and Steve would have a wife. My thoughts turned to marriage. I hoped Mother and Steven would make their marriages spiritual ones. Marriage, not only for security, but for spiritual promise as well. Marriage that would satisfy the soul.

In a spiritual union I thought that neither man nor woman should become a matt. Both should share equally in nurturing life. I wondered about my marriage to John. I had loved him, but I could have shared more of my ideas and thoughts with him. And he could have been a more articulate husband, if I had allowed it. A spiritual union takes two people to make a marriage work. I had learned much from John. But now, I had to create a new life for myself. There were many attitudes that I needed to change even though it was difficult to realize that it was I that needed to do the changing.

I wanted to change the world, but I could only do that by changing my way of thinking and doing. I needed to cut off the negative thinking and replace it with new programs. I truly wanted to change, but I'd have to work on it daily. I would love more and feel more by thinking of how to help others. By doing this, it would help me get my mind off my problems. I felt determined at that moment to live every day abundantly. After all, my heart still pounded passionately in my breast, brain waves still circulated.

And I was informed enough to realize that every day was a gift—a celebration of life. I would grasp every opportunity to live life to its fullest instead of simply rolling over on my back waiting to die. New Year's Day would come and go for me, for all people. But at this point I realized I had the ability to choose my own path, march out carrying the torch. I could make things happen or shrivel up like an autumn leaf and blow away in the wind.

Sophie, can you believe that Steve came home? And that he's getting married. Of course, I've been so involved the past two weeks, planning, getting things ready for the big day of his wedding. I didn't want to let my brother out of my sight. We have had many long talks off and on since he's been staying with me here in Tooele. He's mainly been preparing plans for the wedding. And he's also been to Mother's house a couple of times.

I needed his strength, his insights, and his words of encouragement. There are still questions I ask which have no answers. I think and ponder in my mind and wonder what about my life? Is it real or imagined? I wonder: is this merely a dream world we live in? What is real? All men will die; it is true. But the soul lives on. I believe I can overcome obstacles if I decide to overcome them. Two words keep coming to mind, *carpe diem*. I needed to seize the day, but I needed to seize the day with a larger eternity in mind. Yes, that's the answer. I must. Well, dear, some things have changed to a very great extent, but for now I must attend to those matters that no one has fixed. *Adieu*, dear friend.

As always, Sophie

SATURDAY APRIL 27

Dear Sophie,

It has been a week to remember. I sit here at my kitchen table writing a sentence or two, then pausing to stare at a dozen fresh roses on the table. *Fire and Ice* roses. Exquisite roses! But back to my story in its proper sequence. I will tell you now that Mother and Walter were married the same day as Steve and Angelique. Now the grand double wedding is over, though we have enough leftover chicken crepes to last until the next millennium. Steve has been wonderful. The time he spent here with us the past few months has been enjoyable as well as entertaining. He has been very supportive.

Well as you can imagine, Mother has been on a cloud in body and soul. As to Walter, I can't speak highly enough of him. He is a man of character, gentleness, and love.

But I must return to the time of that horrible day in January, the point at which my story opened. If you recall, it was January 16 on a Tuesday, back in Salt Lake City. That was the evening that the unknown lunatic chose to run me down with his car. There I was in Salt Lake County where I ended up in a hospital there. When I regained consciousness, opened my eyes, I didn't even know where I was.

Prior to January 16, my life had become dream-like. My husband gone, my brother returned to life, two new men come into my life. Certainly, following New Year's Day, I had barely established a regular routine again. Shane was back in school. Steve was in and out, mostly out of the house. Angelique also was staying with us, creating more warm exciting moments. And I? I had gotten out the drafting table and was doing a little drawing of my dream home, dreaming and drawing as Michael had suggested. Some healing was taking place.

But then the joyous healing was interrupted by the mad dog of a man who had chased me down the road in mid-January. As you will recall, I had driven to the Police Station. And the last thing I remembered was talking to a police officer. I found out later at the hospital that I had fainted right there in front of the officer.

Finally when I woke up in a bed, I glanced out the window and saw snowflakes floating down through the early mists of gray. I heard traffic pulsing along outside. I felt tired and I had no clue where I was. Next I looked around the room. There I saw JoEllen and my mother sitting next to my bed, worried looks on their faces. I glanced back out the window; there was some light so I assumed it to be morning. I knew I felt disoriented, knew I was lying in bed with an IV in my left arm. Was I in a hospital? I wasn't sure what was going on.

I couldn't quite clear the fog from my brain. But a few minutes later when I finally could focus my eyes, I noticed a large bouquet of *Fire and Ice* roses which sat in a vase on the bedside stand. Suddenly the snow stopped and some sunshine peeked out. The flowers became backlit by the sun, rays filtering through the window. The roses in sunlight made an inspiring contrast with the drabness of the walls of the room.

"Mother? Where am I?" I had asked, the startle sounding in my voice. "Where are the boys?"

Mother jumped up, took hold of my hand, "Oh Anne!" she said, "You're all right. The boys are fine. Sandy is taking care of them back at Jo's. She picked them up last night."

"And you're at St. Mark's Medical Center," Jo said in response to my first question. "You fainted and they brought you here,"

I remembered being at the Police Station, "I feel all right. What time is it?

Mother cleared her throat and said, "It's Wednesday morning and you're going to be fine. The people at St. Marks have taken good care of you." There was an edge to her usual manner of speaking.

Was she disturbed about my condition? What was being kept from me? "Why am I here? Other than that I fainted." I ran my hand over the bed sheets. They felt stiff and sterile.

Mother gave a try at smiling, "You gave us a scare, that's all, Anne." She laughed nervously but then burst into tears.

"Jo?" I asked, "What's going on?"

Jo took my hand, "Well," she said, "The officer came this morning to report on the man who chased you." Her hair bounced as she shook her head, moved her hands and shoulders.

"So," I replied, "did that horrible man try to kill me because I was driving too slow? What was he thinking?"

Jo held out her hands, "No one knows. He wasn't thinking. He was crazy. They got him and locked him up."

"Good," I blurted out, "But do I have to press charges?"

"No," Jo said, "He was still harassing cars when they found him. So they caught him in the act." She sounded disgusted with the way people were these days.

"Well," I answered, "The world is crowded with crazy, mean characters like that."

Mother was holding my hand. Jo was still sat on the edge of my bed. Mother said, "Crazy, mean people can cause harm. Her eye twitched, a tear slid down her cheek, once again she cleared her throat and said, "We nearly lost you because of him."

"What? I feel fine. And you said I was fine. Why this IV?" At that moment I had a hunger pang, craved some food. "Also, why am I so hungry?"

Mother tapped her fingers on the bed rail. Her face was ashen, her eyes suddenly wet and frantic looking. They were two dark orbs.

Now I felt the hair on my arms stand up. An electric current surged up my spine. I sat up. "You two are confusing me."

With a tissue in hand, Mother sat dabbing perspiration from her forehead. She breathed heavy like panting, "You hemorrhaged. You lost John's baby!" She sniffed then burst out sobbing. She was at the same time squeezing my hand as if it were a vice grip.

I swallowed hard, let the news sink in. Then I felt anger. Anger at the man who chased me. Anger at myself for being weak. Even anger at myself for being in the wrong place at the wrong time. This lunatic had little regard for human existence. He may not have killed me, but the fact was, he had killed my child! There was a long pause of silence. I closed my eyes, sighed, opened my eyes, ground my teeth together.

Could I accept this tragedy? Hadn't I had enough of dying? What had happened to celebrating life? I pressed my fingers against my forehead, tried to smooth the pain away. I took a deep breath, exhaled. I could hear the soft clicking of the IV pump. I felt burning inside with rage. And this sterile hospital setting, I despised it! Death had walked in to look at me, taken my baby, then walked back out. A lump came to my throat. My eyes burned. But I didn't cry. I could think of nothing, as though my mind was blank. Something inside me was stirring. Perhaps it was my heart. I, who had always been too reluctant to let my heart cry out—was now full of the sound of my heart's out-crying. Was it too soon?

I gave a final deep sigh, closed my eyes. I had to try to clear my head. I needed rest. I felt as though I had been run over. I tried to find a peaceful thought that could drive the sorrow away. I thought of Mother and Steve, both of them getting married. They would be married in April.

I told myself these two had weddings coming up in just three months. There was the renewed life I could celebrate. Not my own, but my mother's and Steve's.

Mother held my hand tight.

"Tell me about new life, Mother."

She tried also to dry her tears. Would she tell me about her new life to come with Walter?

"I, tell YOU about new life?" she asked. She seemed startled.

"Yes, tell me about your looking forward to your new life with Water. Tell me about Steve's new life with Angelique!"

Mother dried her tears. She bit at her lip, closed her eyes as she spoke tapping into the inner most parts of her soul, "Almost all new life is the same—if it's really new life. Everything is budding, coming forth. So for Steve and Angelique, that is the way it is." She opened her eyes to relay her final thought, "But you mustn't concentrate on such things now."

I squirmed a bit in bed and told her, "Why? Because there is no 'new life' for me any more?"

"Of course not," Mother replied. "But, at this moment you are suffering from a loss, you have to calmly take that and accept it for what it is. I mean that is the only way to benefit from the troubles God has sent you."

"That is true," Jo said. "You can't know what new life awaits you. But you have to recognize your loss to get to the next phase."

"Yes, I think I understand that," I told Jo, and Mother too. "Maybe all my life I've been more gushing and less realistic than I thought I was. From the spiritual point of view, I guess I've always taken too much comfort in the physical, practical positives in my life." With this I patted Mother on the knee. "Haven't we all done this—at least to an extent and once in a while, at least?"

Again Mother nodded. Her face lit up, "Yes. All human beings do it. I've rejoiced over the material, social good that has come to me from gaining new life for myself by way of Walter. I need to concentrate more on the spiritual aspects of my relationship with Walter."

"Well, yes," I told Mother, "I see what you mean. There is a spiritual way of seizing the day."

"Oh, you two," Jo said. "I think we all have grasped this point."

"Yes, yes," Mother said finally with a chuckle, as she dabbed the tears from her eyes.

Jo said, "Yes, now let's get back down to earth. Isn't Angelique just the finest girl you have ever met? Anne, I know you've been through hell, but we need to get going on some of the details for the weddings." She snapped her finger. "We need to get all the material so we can make those stunning heart-shaped centerpieces for the tables. How's that for a great idea?"

We planned for the new life futures all ready set in motion right there in that hospital room. Wedding bells would soon be ringing from the church tower. It sounded a bit complicated, since both Walter and Mother decided to get married the same day as Steve and Angelique—a double wedding in Salt Lake City. It would be a novel arrangement and so exciting.

Once I was out of the hospital, Sophie, I devoted myself to planning and arranging for the grand event. There was so much to do, to procure, to manage. At that point there was to be a double reception. There would be an open house in Idaho held for Mother and a special one in Tooele for Secret Service friends of Angelique's and Steve's for the new couple.

The whole new affair kept me humming like a bee. It helped to keep my mind active and away from dwelling on my losses. And even then the boys seemed thrilled with the activities and wanted to pitch in. The double wedding itself was to be held at the Old Meeting House on Highland in Salt Lake City—a setting that would ensure the event would be an elegant affair.

Naturally, I threw my energy into helping Mother be fitted for a new wedding dress. My seamstress, Mrs. Faust, who lived down the road, would see to it that Mother would be ready and fashionably attired. Everything occurring was exciting and invigorating.

So, then, Sophie, the wedding day fell on Thursday. It just happened this week and that's why it's still fresh in my mind. The day of the wedding, caterers stood attending to food, frills, and decoration.

JoEllen, Kathy, and I put the red and white centerpieces on the tables for the reception. I made sure Steve's bow tie was straight. His best man, Robbie Tyler from Chicago was looking sharp. Walter's son-in-law, Jesse, was his best man. What a gathering, populated as it were by family members, friends, and old acquaintances of both couples.

Mother looked sensational in her white mid-calf silk and lace overlay dress. Her silver hair was set in curls and lovely. Her dark eyes sparkled enthusiastically. Walter radiated, all dressed up in a silver tuxedo with matching cummerbund. Steve had trimmed his dark hair into a smart cut and his square jaw and prominent nose were softened by his dimples and full lips. He resembled an angel with a suit that matched Walter's. I kept gazing at him thinking, *is he real? or a vision that would disappear once I looked away?*

As to Angelique's, her long wedding gown sparkled with lace, lace, and more lace. Pearl-studded beads set off the bodice of her dress. She looked exquisite, with her perfect features, petite stature, and sweet crooked smile. The groomsmen were handsome in their fine tuxedos with cummerbunds, and bow ties.

The bridesmaids were dressed in Valentine's red dresses with red and white hearts intertwined in their hair like a crown and cascading curly white ribbons streaming down on one side. Large red and white hearts adorned the walls. And then, huge bouquets of red and white balloons were arranged into an arch on the platform. Six huge bouquets of red and white roses stood near the front where the ceremony would take place. My heart raced along with all the excitement, and roses scented the air.

When at last, this great day arrived, the old Meeting House was filled with decor and fine classical music of a small orchestra. The orchestra strings were playing some Paganini and Mozart, then moved into a couple of Vivaldi concertos. And these were intermixed with contemporary love songs. Can you hear it all Sophie? It was a splendid setting.

The wedding was to start at 11:00 a.m. I attended to absorb all the sights, sounds, smells, tastes, and feelings presented there. The atmosphere was joyous, charged by animated guests catching up on the latest news. Eyebrows were raised, necklines were lowered and the scent of fresh cut roses co-mingled with some of the latest perfumes and colognes.

The orchestra continued playing from its repertoire. Then a harpist plucked the wedding song strings. The clock struck eleven signaling the beginning of the grand ceremony. Then, Pachelbel's *Cannon in D* began to play starting off softly like an angel's whisper.

Mother stood ready to stroll up one aisle, Angelique to stroll up the other aisle. Tears sprang to my eyes again. I tried to dab them away with a hanky I kept in my purse.

I was sitting on the second to the front row on the outside with the boys on the inside. At that moment, an electric feeling encompassed my soul. I was somehow compelled to turn and look toward the entryway.

That's when I saw Michael stepping inside the building. The sun streaming in the open door backlit his golden brown hair. A radiant aura surrounded him. He caught my gaze and I waved. He quickly swept in and sat down beside me. Walter let out an audible sigh on the stage.

I felt comforted by the fact that Michael had arrived. I patted his hand and whispered, "We wondered if you would make it on time. I'm certain that Walter is glad you're here."

My lovely friend winked at me and whispered, "How about you?" His snapping blue eyes seemed full of mischief.

I said nothing, just smiled. I thought it better to stay silent in view of the event unfolding. But this question as to how I was, when before he was sitting beside me in on the bench? Back when I was in the hospital? I had been wretched but now I felt wonderful and tingly all over.

I had to recognize and admit the effect of his presence on me, now and in all the times before. I looked at him, studied his handsome features, caught the scent of his delicious cologne, eyed his neatly trimmed nails, his proper fashionable clothing, his fine well-polished dress shoes.

I made every effort to keep my attention on the double-wedding couples, but in all honesty, I was distracted, filled with both calm and excitement because Michael was sitting next to me.

I looked over at my boys. They had a pad of paper on which they eventually could play games or write notes if the ceremony were to go on too long. They were well equipped for the ceremony, thus, they didn't demand my immediate attention.

I wanted to thank Michael for the *Fire and Ice* roses he'd sent to me in the hospital. I carefully pulled a piece of paper from Ben's grasp and took hold of his pencil.

Ben wondered what I was doing.

I whispered in Ben's ear, "I need a piece of paper." Suddenly the music stopped. I took a deep breath. Ben handed a piece of paper to me.

Michael's leg next to mine felt muscular and warm. I bit my lip, tried to concentrate on the ceremony. The audience chuckled at a joke I'd missed. I surmised that a marriage ceremony like this didn't occur daily. That had to be the point of the humorous remark I had not heard.

I scribbled a note and handed it to Michael. I brushed his hand gently to get attention. He raised his brows to indicate that he wondered what I was doing so I wrote on the outside of the note, "Michael."

He grinned and carefully accepted the note, his fingers grasping it. He unfolded it and read, *Thank you so much for the lovely roses you sent me while I was in the hospital.* He raised one eyebrow and looked over at me and then the two boys. He turned his palm up, motioned for my pen. I passed him the pen. He thought a moment, scribbled a note in return. As he wrote, I lifted my face toward the ceremony to hear the words being said.

Mother was married first. I was so thrilled with her acceptance of Walter. I could think only of how happy she acted and how they were going to live together in Idaho. She was going to sell her house and they would be moving away. And Walter planned to build their dream house with Michael's help. How exciting! How wonderful. I realized that I too had grown to love my Mother's partner, and Steve's partner. And what about Michael?

Michael handed me a note. It read, *You're welcome. Will you be mine?*

My ears and face flushed crimson as I read the note. I felt there was no place to hide now. I hardly dared to look at Michael as he handed the pen back to me and winked. Was he serious? He'd said once he was unlucky in love. I had always been lucky in love. I hadn't realized until that moment that in the brief time we had visited between Thanksgiving and Christmas, Michael had become an indispensable part of my life. I felt like I had always known him.

At that moment, time stood still. I wanted to write something significant or impressive. I collected my thoughts, scribbled on the paper and handed it back to Michael. The new couples seemed to be getting a lot of advice before they could say, "I do."

He took the note and read, *YES! When?*

I felt like I had finally overcome my darkest hour. I would seize the day.

Michael wrote another line, placed the paper between two of my fingers.

The note read, *How about a December alliance?* I had to think about it a while. I looked up, Mother was getting ready to say, "I do." She started to cry so hard I didn't think she'd be able to get the words out. Then something so lovely took place that I'll never forget it.

Walter took Mother by the hand and knelt in front of her on one knee. He said, "I would like everyone here to know that Abigail Ross is an angel. I will love her forever and cherish her always." He kissed Mother's hand and stood up. Then the two hugged each other in a tender embrace. Tears stained my cheeks once again.

Michael handed me a tissue, gently took my hand. His hand felt warm, electric. A current of love flowed from his hand to my hand. This force was igniting my whole being. I traced a pattern on the back of Michael's hand with my free hand. I felt as though I was forming a union made in paradise and I wondered if I were a stranger in paradise. Was this a dream? I had dreamed, but hadn't dared let it be so. But this was really happening. That's when I realized that I was the woman in my dream at Christmastime. I was the one who was waltzing with Michael! I wanted to tell the world Anne Ross Olson was going to seize this moment.

Ben had seen Michael take my hand, so he wanted to hold my hand too. He put a tiny hand on top of ours and he laid his head in my lap like a contented kitty. Shane wondered what was going on. My heart was thumping along so wildly I wondered if everyone else could hear it.

Shane was interested in what I was doing. He smiled at me, raised his eyebrows and winked at Michael.

Finally, at the front of the room, Steve and Angelique stood and made wedding vows. They looked radiant and seemed to fit perfectly. As soon as Steve and Angelique had exchanged rings and sealed their love with a kiss, the musicians revived and struck up a lively number. The harpist added a flurry of angelic notes.

The music made me think of John. I suddenly felt like a child caught with her hand in a stashed candy jar. Then I recalled the dream when John had appeared to me. So I knew then that John would smile on this union. John wanted me to be happy.

I wrote a note back to Michael. *Where do you want to live?*

In our dream house, he wrote back. Then he borrowed another paper from Ben and quickly constructed a ring and drew a heart on the top with the initials B.M.W. & A.R.O. He slipped it on my finger and whispered, "Will you be my Valentine?" His hot breath on my ear tickled. I nearly burst out laughing. At that moment, Mother and Walter came floating down the aisle toward us.

I jumped up, hugged both of them. My Secret Agent Man brother stood surrounded by his throng of friends and well-wishers for Angelique. Ben and Shane had run to hug their new aunt and their Uncle Steve. Michael stood up. Then as soon as Mother and Walter had passed on down the aisle, Michael reached for me, embraced, and kissed me. I felt exhilarated and faint simultaneously.

The crowds seemed to disappear. I could only see Michael, and I needed a little fresh air.

I understood now how deeply Michael felt for me. I understood what was happening, what had happened to him, to me, to us.

He took my hand and led me down to the alcove and said, "Anne, will you marry me? I will be lucky in love if you consent."

"Oh, Michael! Does your grandfather know about this?"

"Yes. We have discussed my love for you, my desire to marry you more than once."

I was thrilled, yet moved to tears over such a declaration.

Michael touched my hair with his hand. He twisted a strand around his finger. "You are my special love. I've been looking for you a long time."

A warm calm sensation filled me. Michael was saying such beautiful words to me. I stared at his hands. "I didn't want to accept the feelings I felt for you at first."

"But, Anne, I knew the moment I first saw you, that one day you'd be mine, that you'd accept me. It was written in the stars. You are my love from the beginning and for always."

"And you are the love I crave," I told him. "I have been looking for you my whole life long. With you, I can survive physically but, equally, I can grow spiritually. And my boys all ready love you."

"Do you want me to ask them if I may marry you?"

"They all ready love you, as I said. But how nice to ask them. Yes, you must."

"And are we forever and ever?"

"Yes. But where will our forever be? In Texas? In Utah?"

"How about Idaho? We can be near Mother and Granddad and we'll build our own house." He kissed me on the lips, once, twice, held me close in an embrace for a moment.

It felt so heavenly to have his strong arms around me. Like a dream but real. Suddenly someone pinched my are from behind. It was Steve with a scowl on his face, "So Sis, who's this unidentified man?" he asked in a suspicious manner.

"This is Bradley Michael Wellington, Walter's Grandson. Michael, this is my brother, Steve. He has come back from the dead," I said.

"Who?" asked Steve.

Still holding Michael's hand, I whispered to Steve, "I'm going to marry him."

"What?" Steve looked puzzled a moment, then he said, "I don't even want to hear about it. Another shocker; I may faint." He suddenly shook Michael's hand and good naturedly said, "Good to meet you Brother Michael." He grinned which showed his dimples. "I wish you every happiness in this world."

Michael was standing close to me and said, "Thank you, Brother Steve."

"Let us know about your wedding plans," Steve added, "If this isn't just an 'April Fool's wedding gag, Sis." Then he hurried off to join Angelique.

Mother and Walter appeared with Ben and Shane. Mother seemed a bit fatigued but happy. "I'm sailing on a cloud, but ready for bed."

Michael looked at me, raised one eyebrow, and with only his lips moving, said, "I also." He and I both laughed.

"What's happening here?" Mother asked.

"Michael and I are getting married," I replied.

"Yes, yes," Walter said knowingly shaking his head in hearty approval.

"Married," Mother exclaimed, then sighed.

"Oh, yes, Mother. Rejoice with me."

"I do. I will," Mother said a bit stunned, while letting the reality of this news sink in.

And with that, Michael led me out the main doors into the dazzling light. The trees, flowers all swayed in the gentle breeze. The warm sunlight caressed every living thing igniting life to the surroundings.

I felt vibrantly alive. "When are you flying back to Texas," I asked Michael. There was a dramatic pause while he brushed the overgrown bangs from my eyes.

"I'm not going back. I'm staying in Grantsville with my aunt so I can see you every day. We have some talking to do. We can decide on dates and times later."

Oh, Sophie, Michael has thought through many things. He has planned things with me and the two boys as he has clearly focused many ideas in his careful architect's mind. I look forward to every second of my forthcoming life with this man. My fine, noble prince! Things mundane and super-mundane will be glorious.

Now it was time that we would design and build our dream house. We would have a darkroom where I could develop my own film. We would have shelves and shelves of books and quiet gardens to walk through in meditation, lofty thought and prayer. We'd live out our dreams together living and loving. In the meantime, I wasn't about to take my life for granted. I had seized the day and overcome discouragement by genuinely loving the qualities and virtues of a marvelous man. I could hardly wait to get on with celebrating my life and his, both of us seizing the day, every day!

So now you know how I've matured quite a bit Sophie. I can hear you say, "Anne, it wasn't that you've grown so much as you have returned to your real self again." Yes, it's true. But I'm not sorry for the roads I have journeyed up until now. I have learned from those years, learned of virtues I have helped to grow, virtues I have let go to waste. I see my imperfections but have a new respect for my love of perfect ways.

Yet, my dear Sophie, for now I must bid you *adieu*. As you can see, I have taken on new dimensions, I feel new passions. I love you, dear friend. Thank you so much for your inspiration and words of understanding and for your ever-listening heart. I hope to see you this year. I want you as my witness to the higher life I strive to move on to. I want you as witness not only to my intentions and hopes, but also to the man I have chosen as my mate to be with me along this higher journey; I want to see you smiling benevolently on Michael and me as we walk toward the altar of union. I will be sure, then, and secure in the faith that he and I will make that lofty climb to the realization of our hope of grace and love in the presence of God everlasting.

As ever yours,

Anne

* 9 7 9 8 8 9 3 8 9 1 7 0 6 *